IT'S NOT FOREVER, IT'S FOR NOW

Young in Love
Book 5

ELLE WRIGHT

Elle Wrights Books, LLC
Ypsilanti, Michigan
www.ElleWright.com

Copy Editor/Proofreading:
Melissa Ringsted
There For You Editing

Cover Design:
Sherelle Green

It's Not Forever, It's For Now

A lie can follow you to death.

The first time my mother told me that, it didn't resonate. I'd made it a point to always tell the story that suited me in the moment. Truth or fiction. Except... I didn't count on the lies I told myself. Or the woman who held up the mirror so I could see them.

I'm Tristan... and I got next.

Dear Reader

Tristan got next!!

Every so often, a character latches on to me and won't let go. All of the Youngs have been like this, but Tristan … He was something different. Tapping into his mind, dealing with his trauma, with his hurt, was tough.

Finding him the perfect forever love was quite a journey too. Many of you thought that he'd end up with Demi, but I knew that she wasn't for him. Sasha was. She was the only woman for Tristan.

And their journey … the way they came together was as crazy as it was destiny.

Thank you for your continued support. I hope you enjoy the ride!

Love,

Elle

www.ellewright.com

Content Notes

Hi again,

I love to be surprised when I read a book. But I fully recognize that every reader is not like me. If you haven't read an Elle Wright book before, I feel like I should let you know a few things before you dive in.

IT'S NOT FOREVER, IT'S FOR NOW contains sexual content, profanity, and sensitive subjects that some may find triggering.

Trigger Warnings include but are not limited to:

Death of a parent (mentioned)
Violence
Abusive parent
Toxic relationship
Domestic abuse
Child abandonment
Humiliation

Content Notes

Family estrangement
Grief

For all the baddies. You know who you are.

Where It Started

Prologue

Tristan

A Long Damn Time Ago

*A*ll the warning signs were there. I knew the tools. Anger management had been ingrained in me from the time I could talk. Impulse control, coping skills, breathing exercises, calming activities, books. My father taught me that self-discipline would pay off in spades down the line. I never really believed him. Until now. *It might be too late.*

"What the hell did you do?"

My brother's voice filtered through the rage now simmering to a dull ache in my gut. I felt him move past me and finally my eyes were able to focus on the consequences of my actions. The man was sprawled out on the floor, his blood pooling in the ridges of the hard wood.

Glancing at me, my brother shook his head. I couldn't read his eyes, though. Most would react with horror at the sight. But not Duke … He was a master at the poker face, which infuriated me because he'd learned it from me and somehow surpassed me in skill, even at fourteen years old. It wasn't horror. Not even disgust. Disappointment? Pity?

He ran a hand over his face. "I'm not going to ask what you were thinking because I'm not even sure you know. But Demi can't see this."

Demi.

Tonight she'd come to us in need of help. She'd made a life decision, choosing freedom from her father in the middle of a torrential thunderstorm. A crack of thunder sounded in the distance, signaling the storm outside had passed. But a new one had started inside the moment my fist connected with Mr. Strong's jaw. I didn't *just* keep that muthafucka away from Demi. I'd essentially committed an act of assault on a grown-ass, family court lawyer with connections in high places. Demi's father knew people. He knew judges.

Closing my eyes, I tried to think of a solution. Unfortunately, I was out of good options. Or excuses. "Help me pick him up," I ordered Duke quietly, keeping my eyes glued to the man on the floor.

Duke stared at me incredulously. "Nah, man. That's not what we're going to do."

"Just do it!" I snapped.

Dropping his head, Duke rubbed the back of his neck. "The way I see it, Mom left you in charge. You handle that."

"Then get the fuck out of here!"

Duke didn't hesitate. He headed toward the staircase.

Only he didn't go upstairs. Instead, he turned to face me. "Real talk … You can't pretend you didn't almost kill him like you pretend you're not my brother."

The comment caught me off guard. I can't say I didn't deserve his ire. My behavior lately had put a strain on all my relationships. I'd always known I was different, but nights like this cemented the notion. Duke stayed in trouble, but he thought like *his* father. Because the man who taught me everything, the man who wouldn't hesitate to take a bullet for me, wasn't *my* real father. He was my uncle. And the woman who'd nursed me back to health when I was sick and put me to sleep every night with the sweetest rendition of "Baa Baa Black Sheep" I'd ever heard wasn't my mother. I wasn't even related to her at all. While they'd given me all the assurances that I was part of them, I didn't feel like it. Of their eight kids, I was the outlier. I wasn't destined for college. I hated school. I preferred solitude over crowds. Football was my sport, but I wasn't really a team player. Several of my siblings were probably going to follow the example set and become therapists. But they would make money helping people like me.

Sighing, Duke said, "Maybe you should just call Mom and Dad."

"If you're not going to help, leave," I whispered.

"If you won't do it for me, do it for Demi. She's already scared enough. Mom and Dad will know what to do."

Of course they would. Stewart and Victoria Young made a living knowing what the hell to do. They'd built an empire teaching others how to do the same. Growing up, I had never really appreciated their background in psychology. Mostly, I'd considered it my trap. Because I couldn't escape them. They seemed to know every tactic I used to get out of trouble or avoid communicating. All they'd ever done was given me a family, a place to call home. My imperfections, my mood swings, my expectations, my bull-shit … None of it ever mattered to them. And as crazy as it sounded, I'd resented it—resented *them*. Now I needed them.

Duke muttered a low curse. "At some point, you have to realize that you fucked up. You need help. In more ways than one. And this?" He gestured to the bloody man. "This shit isn't going away."

I stepped over to the man and bent low, once again checking his pulse. "I need to get him out of here. Help me lock him in the guest room."

"What type of rock you been smokin', man? Accessory to kidnapping is not in my life plan. I'm not moving shit."

Mr. Strong groaned softly. "Demita," he mumbled, calling for his daughter. As if the sound of his own voice jarred him awake, the older man swung, throwing frantic air punches. He rolled around on the ground, trying to stand.

My brother glared at me. "This is some fucked up shit. Your ass is going to jail."

"You're done," Mr. Strong threatened, finally standing upright. "I'll ruin you."

As far as I was concerned, I was already ruined. But I wasn't going out like a punk. Before I could dig myself further into a shallow grave by kicking that asshole to the ground again, Duke's hand on my arm stopped me.

"Actually, *you* came to *our* house and tried to swing on him." He shrugged. "You were a physical threat—screaming like a crazed lunatic outside of our home in the middle of a thunderstorm, banging on the door, barging into the house uninvited as soon as he opened the door, and destroying my mother's antique vase in your haste to enter. I'm scared for my fourteen-year-old life," he dead-panned, indicating that he was the opposite of frightened but would make it work if the police asked about it. "My brother used reasonable force to protect himself, his minor brother, and *your* daughter who obviously was running for her life to get away from you. She's a bruised, bloody mess. You're an attorney. Sounds like self-defense to me."

I blinked, meeting my brother's unbothered gaze. The only thing I could do in that moment was nod in agreement. Duke always had the gift of gab. He could talk to anyone and remembered everything he read.

Mr. Strong's shoulders fell on a muttered curse. He looked at me. "You won't get away with this."

Duke pushed past him and opened the front door. "That's nice. Get the fuck out of here before I'm forced to defend *myself*."

The long moment that passed as we all stood in the foyer seemed like an eternity, but Mr. Strong finally grabbed his shit and bounced.

Shaking his head, Duke said, "Do the right thing, Tristan?" Then he disappeared up the stairs.

Without a word, I walked over to the phone my parents kept in the hallway and dialed the number. When my father answered, I blew out a deep breath. "Dad, I messed up. When will you get here?"

An hour passed and I was seated on a bench in the foyer. I'd already checked on Demi, and she seemed fine with Duke. The smeared blood on the floor had darkened as it dried. My instinct to clean had been doused by my father's instructions to "not touch anything."

The sound of the back door opening drew my attention to the kitchen. Silence. Unlike every other time my family returned home. When the Young family entered a room, there were always loud voices, silly laughter, and annoying arguments. But there was nothing. No sound. My mother wasn't yelling for Asa to pick up his shit. Dallas wasn't telling everyone else what to do. Blake wasn't cussing anyone out. *Nothing.*

Seconds later, my "father" walked in the foyer. Assessing the damage, he picked up a shattered piece of Ma's vase and sighed.

I swallowed past a hard lump in my throat, fighting the tears that threatened to fall. Despite everything, the truth was … I was relieved. Grateful. Seeing him walk into the door somehow made things better.

"Where is everybody?" I whispered.

He ignored me as he paced the area again, running his thumb over the thick glass in his palm. "In the car," he answered. "They'll be in when I give them the okay." Finally, he met my gaze. "Are you alright?"

"I blacked out," I explained. "He was shouting, threatening Demi. I couldn't stop …"

"I'm not going to beat you down tonight, but you've created a problem that needs to be handled."

"I defended myself," I argued lamely. It was the truth, but it wasn't the entire truth. The part of me that enjoyed the feel of my fist against that man's jaw, the part of me that loved seeing fear in that man's eyes … Although I liked to think I would've stopped myself, I wasn't so sure. Duke saved my life that night. And I hated him just as much as I was grateful for him.

Dad waved a dismissive hand my way. "I'm not worried about Alan Strong, son." He stood in front of me, prompting me to stand because I hated to not be on the same level as anybody. "Your anger has spiraled out of control. I've tried to allow you the space to find yourself, but I cannot allow you to disrupt this family anymore."

Over the years, I'd done plenty to destroy my relationship with my family. Fights at school, weeks-long suspensions, expulsion. I'd gone to three different high schools until I finally settled down enough to graduate. But …

Would he really make me leave?

"Are you kicking me out?" I asked incredulously. "For this?"

Squeezing my shoulder, Dad shook his head. "No. Never. And you know this, but—"

"Stew?" Ma called from the kitchen. "Baby, are you …" Her voice trailed off as she entered the foyer. "What the hell happened?" Gasping, she rushed over to me and touched my jaw with her soft palm. That small gesture was like a balm over rough, cracked skin. Over my heart. "Are you okay, babe?"

I stepped away from her, away from the contact. "I'm fine."

She wasn't deterred, though. Instead of taking the hint, she stepped closer, brushing her thumb against my chin the way she'd always done. "Did he hurt you?"

The realization that she wasn't mad at me, but concerned about me, was too much for me in that moment. I didn't deserve this. *I don't deserve her.* "Please stop," I mumbled. "I'm fine."

"Your father told me what happened," she continued. "I'm worried about you, son."

Her words seemed to ignite the fire of anger inside of me again. Because I wasn't *her* son. She knew it. I knew it. "Stop touching me!" I snapped, pushing her away.

Before I could say anything else, though, my father hemmed me up against the wall, feet off the ground. "We're not doing this, Tristan" he warned. "Not today. Not ever. I will put my foot up your ass if you disrespect my wife again."

"It's okay, Stew," Ma said, her voice soft, calm. "I'm fine."

Dad stared at Ma, but his thick hand remained around my neck. "Can you give us a minute?"

Ma glanced at Dad, then back at me. But she didn't argue. She tossed me one last backwards glance and left.

Once she disappeared into the kitchen, Dad's furious glare met my eyes. He squeezed my neck gently, but firmly. "Don't try me, son. My fists still work, and you know I know how to use them."

I'd always heard stories about Dad as a young man. And I'd seen him in action myself a time or two. Despite the money and prestige he had now, life hadn't always been that way for him. He needed to fight his way through his childhood and had never forgotten where he came from. Everything he had today, he'd earned it with hard work and perseverance.

"I've had it with your bullshit." He squeezed my neck gently but firmly.

When he finally let go, I slumped to the floor. "I'm sorry," I grumbled.

Dad stretched his neck. "Last time we talked, you mentioned that you'd reached out to a recruiter."

I remembered the conversation we'd had right before they left town. The tense discussion had centered around my declaration that I had no intention of going to college and wanted to join the military. Dad and Ma had tried to convince me to take a different path, maybe pursue a trade or even join a police force. But I'd fought them because I felt that I needed to find my own way.

"Don't worry about cleaning up," Dad continued. "I'll take care of it. And I'll handle Demi and her father." He squeezed my shoulder. "The first step to healing is realizing you're sick. It's time for you to do the work. All that anger and resentment you carry will weigh you down until it takes you out."

The tears standing in Dad's eyes triggered my own. The first one streaked down my cheek, and I made no move to wipe it away. "I will do better," I promised.

He flashed a sad smile. "I don't want to see you destroy yourself or anyone else for that matter. I love you, but since you insist on 'finding your own way,' call the recruiter in the morning."

Dad pulled me in for a tight hug. Then, he left. And as I stared around the space, once again taking in the damage I'd caused, sadness threatened to choke me with its intensity. Glancing up, I noticed Duke standing on the landing in the hallway upstairs. The disappointment in his eyes was clear even from that distance, but he didn't speak. He simply walked away.

Now, it's time for me to do the same.

Chapter One

A TRISTAN YOUNG ORIGINAL

Tristan

The Week Before Thanksgiving, Several Years Ago

Someone once called me a victim. I'd been called many things, but that was the worst. I hated that shit. Hated the way it made me feel. Helpless. Defeated. So I went out of my way to be the villain in every situation—until I learned that sometimes the best reaction was inaction. I worked to avoid my triggers. Unfortunately, that meant limiting my interaction with people who made me want to lash out—even if it was my family.

The best thing I ever did was call that recruiter. Enlisting had changed my trajectory from potential inmate to entrepreneur. My time away had also prepared me to step into the most important role of my life—father. My six-year-old daughter was everything to me. She didn't care about my past. She didn't think about my future. She just loved me. And becoming Raven's daddy had saved my life, made me want to be better. I wasn't about to fuck that up for just anybody. No matter how good the pussy felt to me.

"What do you think?"

I glanced up at the woman perched on top of me, her naked body still wet from the shower we'd just taken together. We met at a mutual friend's barbecue months ago and spent the night talking shit to each other on the Spades table. And when her and her partner had lost the tournament, my dick helped her forget that crushing defeat in a basement closet. Britt Nelson was a mystery, though. Unlike other women I'd encountered, she kept the details of her life under lock and key. She never made demands for my time. She told me from jump that she wanted my dick, not my heart. When she needed to get fucked, she called me.

Tonight was different. For the first time since we'd met, she revealed to me that she had a son who was a little older than Raven. I wasn't a trusting person by nature, but I'd already done my due diligence on her when we decided to keep fucking. Yet even though I already knew about her son, I didn't want her to get comfortable sharing details about her life with me. Then, when I was balls deep inside of her, ready to come, she caught me off guard and offered me a job. And *that* brought this thing between us to an abrupt halt.

Britt stared at me through hooded eyes. "Well?"

Gripping her hips, I lifted her up and deposited her onto the mattress next to me. "I think it's time for me to go."

She made no move to cover up. "You haven't even heard the proposal."

"I don't need to." I stood and pulled on my jeans. "I can't work for you."

"Even if I paid you twenty thousand dollars?"

I paused, then turned to face her. Money talked. At this stage in my life and career, I had definite goals that required capital to achieve them. Sighing, I leaned against a dresser and folded my arms over my chest. Britt lived a modest life in her three-bedroom home on the west side of Detroit. She married young but lost her husband in a drive-by shooting outside of a club in the city. As a result, she kept her circle small. Aside from her grandmother and her brother, she didn't have any family. The only loyal person she seemed to have in her life was her best friend, Daphne. She wasn't flashy by any means. She dressed down, often wearing jeans, a hoodie, and a pair of Timberlands. Her hair was usually styled in braids or a ponytail. No fake nails. No makeup. She worked long hours at the plant and drove an old F-150. On the other hand, she never mentioned being broke either. Maybe it was just an act?

Or is Britt hiding more than her feelings? Either way, I needed to do what I did best. Find out.

"Where would you get the money?" I asked finally.

Britt yanked her purse from the nightstand and dumped a bundle of cash on the bed. After picking it up, she sauntered over to me and held it up to my nose. "Don't worry about my money. Just know that I have it. And I'll fight to keep it."

Shit. Even as my brain screamed at me to walk away from her, my dick hardened at her display of bravado. That part wasn't an act. One thing I *did* know about Britt?

She would have no problem cracking a bottle over my head and leaving me in a pool of my blood. And I knew this because I had a sister who had zero fucks to give, too.

Britt retreated to the far side of the hotel room where her clothes were neatly folded on a chair. Slowly, she got dressed. "You're not the only one who did their homework," she mentioned casually, glancing at me out of the corner of her eye. "You grew up as the eldest of eight siblings. Your parents … Let's just say I've read all about Mr. and Mrs. Stewart Young. I know about their degrees and businesses just like I know about you. Enlisted right out of high school?" She arched a brow. "Used the skills you were taught by your parents to become a Human Intelligence Officer. Decided to take those skills and start your own PI firm."

Up to that point, she'd kept her eyes trained on me. But then she made her mistake. She dropped the money on the floor and bent to pick it up. That's when I approached her. When she stood to her full height again, I was right in front of her. Still, she didn't retreat. She stepped in closer, until our bodies were touching again.

"You talk too much," I whispered, tracing my thumb down her cheek before I wrapped my hand around her neck. I didn't believe in violence against women, but I also wanted her to know that she didn't run shit up in here. "You already know I don't like to talk."

With her gaze firmly on mine, she gripped my dick in her palm and squeezed. "But *I* want to talk, though. And I have your balls in my hand."

"Is that a threat?"

"No. It's a promise." She sucked my bottom lip into her mouth. A second later, she backed away, and I let her go. "You have one daughter but couldn't make it down the aisle to marry her mother," she continued. "While you get your mail in Ann Arbor, you choose to stay in the city. Is that because you'd rather be anywhere other than with your family? I'm not sure—"

"That's enough," I commanded. "I don't need you to recite my history. Tell me what you want, and I'll tell you if I can do it."

Britt smiled then. But it didn't reach her eyes. She picked up her purse and pulled out a picture. "Find this nigga."

The next week, I sat outside of a local bar and grill in Dearborn, Michigan. Loud thoughts made it hard for me to process what had just happened. Britt's request seemed simple enough, but I sensed there was an inherent danger in it. The last thing I wanted to do was be pulled into some street shit. Which was why I didn't immediately accept the job. Because I knew taking her money would put me squarely in the middle of a war. When I started my business, I figured I'd tap into wealthy clientele looking for someone to gather information on business rivals, husbands and wives who wanted me to catch their cheating spouses in the act, corporations who needed background checks, people searching for missing family members, or attorneys who needed assistance with their case files. Easy shit. Legal shit. Shit that wouldn't land me in a morgue or force me to put someone in a grave.

My phone buzzed, interrupting my thoughts, and I smiled at the phone number displayed on the screen. "Hey, Bubbles."

"Daddy!" Raven screeched, her tiny voice centering me.

I smiled. "What are you doing?"

She let out an exaggerated sigh. "I don't have school

tomorrow. Mommy said it's Thanksgiving. Can you come visit?"

After our breakup, Malika decided to move back to her hometown in Virginia to be close to her parents. I didn't fight her because I knew that her life would be easier if she could have support. Although our relationship didn't last, I respected her as my daughter's mother, and we worked together to co-parent Raven.

"I wish I could come visit, but I'm in Michigan," I explained. "But I'll come get you next month so you can spend Christmas with me."

Out of the corner of my eye, I spotted a woman pacing in front of the door to the restaurant. I catalogued her features, noting her attire. She was covered from head to toe, dressed in all black from her hat to her leather coat to her pants to her high-heeled boots. She wore shades so I couldn't see her eyes. When she glanced at her watch for the third time, I figured she was waiting on someone to show up. And the deep-set frown on her full lips was the only visible sign of her irritation. She paused for a minute, seemingly focusing on something across the street. I followed the movement until my gaze landed on …

Duke?

My brother jogged toward her, giving her a brief hug before he opened the door for her and followed her inside.

"Daddy?" Raven called.

I blinked, forcing myself to focus on my daughter and not my brother or the woman he was with. "Yes, Bubbles."

"Do people fart in Michigan?"

Conversations with my daughter never failed to amuse me. I chuckled. "Yes."

"I farted in Ms. Brown's class, and everyone laughed at me. Mommy said it's normal."

Shaking my head, I told her the same thing. "It's

nothing to be ashamed of. Did you say 'excuse me' after you did it?"

"Yes. But stupid Justin told me my butt stinks."

I didn't want to threaten a first grader, but I also didn't want a dusty-ass little boy to give my daughter a complex either. "Tell Justin your daddy will come and show him—"

"That's enough, Bubbles," Malika interrupted. "Why don't you go wash your hands for dinner? Hey, Tristan."

"What's up, Lika?"

"You know, you can't threaten every little kid that dares to say anything to Raven. And you can't protect her from everything."

"I can try," I countered. "Justin needs to shut the hell up."

Malika laughed. "Whatever. I got the money you sent. You didn't have to send me money to get my car fixed. But thank you."

"Do you need anything else?" I asked.

"No. I found a mechanic that will do the job. My mother is letting me drive her car to work while it's in the shop."

"Good. Well, I'll be down there in a couple of weeks. I have a job lined up in Virginia Beach. I figured I could just head on up to Richmond and drive Raven back to Michigan with me for the holidays."

"Sounds like a plan," Malika said. I heard a loud scream in the background. Malika cursed. "That damn dog just shit on my mother's carpet. Let me go. I'll let Raven call you tomorrow when you're at your parents' house. I promised your mom."

"I may not go over there," I confessed.

Malika let out a heavy sigh. "I wish you would, Tristan. You can't keep running from your family. They love you."

"I love them, too." While we were together, I'd shared

some things about my past with Malika. She'd always encouraged me to mend my relationships with my siblings. As far as I was concerned, there was nothing to fix. Some families weren't close. I loved them, but I didn't need to be around them all the time either. I kept in touch. I visited sometimes. That was it. And I was perfectly content with that. "But I'm not in the mood for a big crowd this year."

"Or any year," she grumbled.

Duke emerged from the restaurant alone. "I heard you," I told Lika.

"I wanted you to hear me," Lika tossed back. "Anyway, I'll talk to you tomorrow."

"Give Raven a kiss from me." I ended the call as I watched my brother walk to his car.

For months now, Duke had been agitated and distant. Not that I'd witnessed this behavior myself. I had seven siblings. Secrets never stayed quiet long. And somehow everybody's business always got back to me. This time, I'd heard everything about Duke and his mysterious behavior from my baby brother, Asa. Apparently, my parents were involved in whatever was going on. My sisters had whispered about it to each other. And my other brother, Dex, had stayed silent. Which was to be expected since he and Duke were identical twins and had always kept each other's confidence. I hadn't given the information much thought because I didn't really care. Duke was a grown man. If he needed help, he'd ask. But now …

In that moment, I went against my instinct to mind my business and got out of my car and made my way to the restaurant. Scanning the small dining room, I spotted the woman at the bar. Decision made, I approached the bar and took the seat next to her.

I watched her through the mirror behind the bar. Up close, she was stunning. Smooth, brown skin. Thick, black hair that fell like waves down her back. Pouty lips. Long legs. And she smelled like daisies wrapped in heartbreak. A dangerous combination that should have sent me right out the door. But I couldn't move. She took a sip of something dark. Bourbon?

The bartender interrupted my musings, leaned in close to her, and asked, "Another Jack and Coke?"

She smiled sadly. "Sure."

"I'll have the same," I announced. The woman faced me finally, staring at me through big, expressive brown eyes. *Damn.* "Put hers on my tab."

Snickering, she shook her head. "No thank you."

She speaks.

Her voice was soft, but there was an edge to the tone. "I don't know you. I don't want to know you."

I held up my hands in surrender. "Got it. No problem."

The bartender paused, his gaze flitting back and forth between me and her. "I'll be right back with your drinks."

With her eyes locked on mine, she asked, "Do you always assume women need you to buy their drink?"

"Not really. Just being nice. I'm new in town."

She arched a brow. "Really? Do you always lie to women when you're trying to pick them up?"

She's good. "What makes you think I'm lying?"

She motioned to the window. "I saw you sitting in your car. Michigan plates."

"What if it's a rental?"

"Is it?"

"No," I admitted. "I figured I'd seem less intimidating if I came off like a clueless visitor."

"No. If anything, you just seem desperate."

"Ouch."

She smirked. "Just kidding. Who are you? Did someone send you here?"

"Tristan. And why would someone send me here?"

Shrugging, she thanked the bartender when he set her drink on the bar. She finished it in one gulp and stood. She assessed me, tilting her head, and her gaze traveled over my face. "Have a good day."

Then she left.

Chapter Two

DICK INFLUENCED

Tristan

Thanksgiving Day, Many Years Ago

$\mathcal{M}$y first memory of my biological mother was also the last. Thanksgiving. The sad part? The only reason I remembered her at such a young age was because she'd answered a simple question that had stuck with me.

"_No, son. The reason you don't see hams running around is because a ham is part of a pig. Remember the sound a pig makes? Oink, oink._"

At three years old, I'd mimicked the sound happily and then focused my attention back to my toy tractor. That story traveled with me through pre-school and kindergarten to elementary school and middle school—always told as a funny Tristan-ism at family events, always shared to new people who wanted to hear everything about me and my siblings. It wasn't until high school that I realized the woman in the story, teaching me about farm animals while I nibbled on a piece of ham, was also the woman who'd given birth to me. And then she died before I could form a meaningful memory of her. A connection to her.

After I found a copy of my original birth certificate, I confronted my parents, and they finally told me the truth. Everything changed for me that day. The realization that "Aunt Sheila" was really my mother had thrown my life into a tailspin of questions with no good answers. It had colored every experience, drawn dark lines through perfectly curated pictures of my family in my head. After that, I never ate another piece of ham again. And I hated Thanksgiving.

Because the only woman I'd ever called "Mom," the only woman who'd been there consistently, the only woman who'd had the power to make me feel big and small with one look in her eyes was Victoria Young. And the man who'd always been "Dad" was actually my real mother's brother, my uncle.

I blamed myself. I blamed my parents. Most of all, I blamed *her*.

The proof was there all along, though, but I'd refused to put the pieces together. Because I was happy. I was loved. That was all that mattered to me then. The two people who raised me had never lied to me about being adopted. I was the one who decided I didn't need to know who my biological parents were, and they'd honored my wish, assuring me that they'd answer any questions I had when I was ready. They'd even told me about Sheila

Young. They'd never kept her from me. At any time, I could open a trunk and find countless photos of her. Graduation pictures. Grainy slides of family barbecues. Dark images of her and "Dad" as kids, running gleefully under sprinklers and shit. Group pics of all of them at parties with wide afros and wide smiles.

Yet once that door was open, once the memory clicked, nothing was ever the same again for me. I started noticing shit. Things about myself, differences between me and my siblings, the way I didn't look like anyone in my family. Viewing everything through a clearer, smarter lens had also revealed clues about Sheila—the sadness in her eyes, the cigarette always dangling from her fingers, the drink sitting next to her on a table. There was never a man with her, only a substance. Her outward beauty masked secrets I suspected no one knew about, experiences she'd gone to lengths to keep buried.

I spent an entire year learning about her, interviewing old friends, reading her journals. She loved her family. She loved to braid hair. She loved to fight. She loved to smoke weed on the roof in the summer. She loved to sing and play cards. She loved men and rarely told them no when they came calling. The things she hated, though ... Those things contributed to her tragic death.

Behind the wide smiles, the bubbly personality, Sheila hated to look at herself in the mirror. She hated herself. She hated healthy food, so she barely ate. She hated the doctor and refused to go for a checkup. In fact, the only time she went to the doctor was when she found out she was pregnant with me. That's also when they discovered the tumor on her colon. Dad had pleaded with her to get treatment, to take care of herself so that she could carry me to term. He'd even offered her money to cover her medical bills, which she'd taken. Fortunately, the surgeon was able to remove the tumor.

The truth was, though … Sheila never wanted me in the first place. Cancer or no cancer. She'd made that very clear when she refused to even hold me after I was born. And when she insisted that they never reveal to me that I was her son. She did continue to take Dad's money, though. She lived her best life for a while, before the cancer returned with a vengeance. By then, I was Tristan Young, not Tristan Morgan. My parents had officially adopted me and the woman who'd given birth to me spent the rest of her life suffering.

Ma spotted me outside on the porch and grinned, waving me inside. "You're here." She pulled me into a warm hung, and I wanted to stay there. When I tried to back away, she held on to me tighter. She had the gift of comfort. Her voice could soothe and restore any wounded soul. I always tried to appear unaffected, but she knew it was a façade. After all, she'd raised me. "I missed you, my son," she whispered against my ear before placing a gentle kiss to my cheek. "Thank you for coming."

Closing my eyes, I allowed myself to relax into her embrace. "I missed you, too," I croaked.

Ma finally let go and quickly put distance between us. I knew she hated to withdraw her love from me, but she'd done it anyway because it's what she thought I wanted. We'd never talked about that fateful night years ago, when Dad almost beat my ass in her honor, but I still remembered what she'd told me before I left for basic training.

"I love you. When you're happy. When you're sad. When you're angry. Nothing can ever change that. I'm your mother. And there's nothing you can do about it. Be safe. My home will always be yours."

She didn't know it, but those words kept me alive during tough times. I'd been able to recall those words—

the inflection in her voice, the image of her face—to give me the strength I needed to make it. And to ensure that I never forgot, she'd wrote the same thing in every letter, every card she'd sent to me while I was away.

Ma flashed a wobbly smile. "I made your favorite this year. Roast beef."

I made it a point not to eat the traditional Thanksgiving turkey because it reminded me of Sheila. So Ma always made something for me, even if she didn't know I'd be there. Groaning, I thanked her. "With extra gravy?"

"You know it," she confirmed.

"Hey, big brother." My sister, Paityn, wrapped her arms around my waist. "I was hoping to see you this year."

Hugging her, I kissed her forehead. "I hope you made peach cobbler."

Paityn had picked up most of Ma's culinary skills. Just like Ma, she poured her heart into every dish she made and genuinely enjoyed cooking for all of us. Although she was two years younger than me, she took on a nurturing role for us. It wasn't uncommon for her to prepare dinner, help the younger siblings with homework, and even mediate arguments in my parents' absence. And she was a damn good listener, too.

"I decided to try my hand at sweet potato pie this year since Duke didn't have time to do them."

The mention of my brother's name brought my mind back to yesterday. "Is he not coming to dinner?"

Paityn glanced at Ma out of the corner of her eye. "He's here. Just busy this year."

I met Ma's gaze, too. "Medical school kicking his ass?"

"You already know." Ma held out her palm. "Pay up."

I let out a heavy sigh and handed her a twenty-dollar bill for The Cussing Jar. Back in the day, it was nothing to toss a quarter or even a dollar into the jar just to be able to say what the hell I wanted. But when Ma upped her price, especially in high school, that little pocket money she took from us would determine whether we were able to go out or stay at home.

Paityn bumped my hip with hers. "Did you find a place in town yet?"

Of all my siblings, I talked to Paityn the most. She had a way of coaxing shit out of me. The last time we spoke, I'd shared with her that I planned to purchase property in Detroit, but I'd stopped myself from giving her too many details. The simple fact that I'd told her that much was enough. I preferred to move in silence and vowed a long time ago to keep my shit to myself, if for no other reason than to be contrary. Truthfully, I had no good reason to be this way, though. Especially since Ma and Dad had given all of us freedom to choose our own paths. But there was just something in me that couldn't let go of my anger at them. And I actively punished them by withholding my life from them. Except for Raven ... I ensured she was able to know them because I knew her life would be better if she were part of this family.

"No," I answered, looking around the massive kitchen. I grabbed a roll from a basket and bit into it. "Where is everybody?"

"Dallas is hiding from Blake and Ma." Paityn giggled. "Before you got here, Ma threatened her with bodily harm after she put sweetened milk instead of evaporated milk into the mashed potatoes."

"Damn," I muttered, running a hand over my chin. "So there's no mashed potatoes?"

Paityn snickered. "You know Ma had another bag. Dallas disappeared, and Blake had to peel them mugs."

"She's pissed," I mused, thinking of my feisty little

sister, Blake. Of all of my sisters, she was the one who liked to fight. "Dallas better run."

"Right?" Paityn agreed. "Bliss is trying to calm Blake down, though. While Demi is on Dallas duty."

Demi. The scared little girl who'd come to our house bloody and bruised had grown into a beautiful woman. One who had haunted my dreams many nights. After the incident, my father had managed to talk Mr. Strong into letting them keep Demi. I wasn't sure what he'd done to convince him, but Demi moved into our house the next day. And she'd never left.

Paityn eyed me knowingly. "She asked about you."

I glanced at Ma, who was now yapping on the phone to someone, before meeting my sister's waiting gaze. "Is she okay?"

Smiling, Paityn nodded. "More than okay."

Cheers erupted from the family room, and my father's distinctive voice pierced the air. "That's what I'm talking about."

"I guess the Lions finally scored one," Paityn offered.

I smirked. "'Bout time." Thanksgiving wasn't just about food in this house. Every year, my father demanded dinner be served *after* the Detroit Lion's game. "Last time I checked, they were losing."

"Still losing," she confirmed.

Shaking my head, I walked toward the door. "I need to see the damage for myself." But before I could leave the room, Demi entered, pausing once she saw me.

Damn. Unable to help myself, I allowed my eyes to rake over her, from her wild, light brown curls to her sock-covered feet. Feelings I'd tried to keep at bay spread from my heart to every other part of my body, coating my tattered insides with hope. Being in her presence was the closest to heaven I thought I'd ever be. She was like sunshine to my cloudy mind, an angel offering redemption. I wanted her.

I don't deserve her.

Demi approached me tentatively. "Hi," she whispered.

My eyes focused on her mouth. "Hey."

"Glad you're here. I was hoping to hear from you last week."

It was clear to me from the moment I'd met Demi as a little girl that she had a little crush on me. While it had started as an innocent best friend's big brother thing, somehow it had morphed into something more. While I was overseas, she'd sent long letters every month, thoughtful gifts, and up-to-date pictures of everyone. She made herself available to me when I came home on leave, often leaving little trinkets on my pillow or having my favorite foods on hand when I arrived. Soon, I realized her love for me wasn't unrequited anymore. And I found myself wanting more of her, needing all of her.

When I met Malika, I figured it was best that I let go of my infatuation for Demi. I'd told myself that she was too young, too innocent to be tainted by me. I'd never forget the hurt in Demi's eyes when I announced that I was going to be a father. But then she'd graciously given me her blessing. In the end, though, I couldn't bring myself to marry Lika knowing she could never measure up. She could never be Demi.

The slow dance between Demi and I continued, but every time we grew close, something inside of me pulled back. But two weeks ago, Demi reached out to ask if I would be in town for the holiday. My need to see her propelled me to ask her to breakfast. Just us. No buffers. I wasn't surprised that she'd happily accepted, but then ... Britt called. Every time we were on the precipice of something deeper, something more meaningful, something official, I fucked it up. That wasn't on Demi, though. It was all me, all my fault.

Demi squeezed my hand. "Can we talk?"

Clearing my throat, I nodded. "Sure."

Demi led me to the library near the front of the house, avoiding Ma and Paityn's curious stares along the way. I sat on the leather bench near the entrance—away from her. She took the hint and took the seat at the desk.

We sat in silence for a moment before she said, "Tristan, I don't want this to be awkward. But I'm wondering why you even asked me out if you weren't going to show up."

Visions of her sitting alone at one of her favorite restaurants taunted me. Because I was there. I'd stood just outside of the window, where she couldn't see me. She was excited, had even pretended to browse the menu as if she would order anything other than her normal pancakes with extra butter and syrup. As the minutes ticked by, I noticed her smile wither into a frown. I watched her discretely wipe away tears from her eyes. And I hated myself for it. Yet, instead of walking inside, instead of giving her the small gift I'd picked up from Belize for her, instead of doing the right thing, I left. And let Britt distract me momentarily.

"Tristan?" Demi called softly.

I met her gaze then. "I'm sorry."

She ran her thumb over the edge of her sweater. "I'm not sure what to say to that."

"Forgive me." Because I couldn't bear her anger. I couldn't live with the fact that I'd hurt her—again. "I should've called."

"You should've been sure," she tossed back. "I just don't know what you want from me."

I stood then, closing the distance between us. I held out

my hand, and when she placed hers on mine, I tugged her to her feet. Searching her eyes, I leaned in, circling her nose with mine. "I want you, but I don't want to hurt you."

Her chin trembled. "But you did."

"I worry that I can never be the man you need me to be, Demi. You're so beautiful. So good. And I'm … not. I don't want to pull you into my darkness."

She brushed her palm over my cheek. "I know who you are."

"I know that you believe that. But you don't. Not really. And us? If things go wrong, it affects everyone."

"When did you start caring about what anyone thinks?"

Closing my eyes, I let out a slow breath. Then I opened my eyes and pinned her with a stare. "I care about what *you* think. And I—"

The front door swung open and Duke stepped into the foyer. He glanced over at us, narrowing his eyes on me. His gaze traveled over to Demi, who fidgeted under his stare. "What's up?"

"Hey," Demi chirped. "You made it back just in time for dinner."

Duke didn't answer her. Instead, he looked at me. "You're here?"

My relationship with Duke hadn't improved over the years. There weren't many people who could knock me off my square, yet he was one of them. Paityn once told us we were too much alike. I figured that was the reason we resented each other.

I eyed my little brother. "Got here a little while ago."

"Hm …" was his response. "Hopefully, you'll stick around long enough to eat the roast Ma cooked for you this year." He shot Demi another short glance before he walked away.

"I'm sorry," she whispered. "He's … going through something."

"What is it?" I asked, my curiosity getting the best of me.

Demi scratched the back of her neck and tucked a strand of hair behind her ear. "Just busy."

Busy. Paityn had said the same thing, but I knew there was more to the story. The question was, did I care enough to find out? He looked normal, but there was a shadow behind his eyes, one that had never been there before. He was still one of the people who could trigger my wrath with one comment.

"If you know something about my brother, tell me. Maybe I can help."

"Trust me. You can't help him right now. And he wouldn't want your help anyway." She sighed. "Besides, he's leaving town for a while to get himself together."

One of the downsides of living on the periphery of the family was I didn't know important shit. I had no idea Duke was even entertaining leaving Michigan. Or what that meant for medical school. Obviously, something had happened to change his trajectory. But no one wanted me to know what that was. Not even Demi.

"This probably isn't the best place to have this talk," Demi said. "Maybe we can try again for breakfast? Tomorrow morning? Before the Black Friday store rush."

I traced the line of her nose and nodded. "Okay."

She grinned, wrapping her arms around me in a tight hug. "I missed you."

Pulling back, I leaned in again, letting myself take in the scent of her shampoo, the mint on her breath. The sound of Dad's booming voice, cursing the Lions to hell and back, jerked me out of the moment and I knew the home team had lost. Again.

Seconds later, laughter filtered into the hallway from the kitchen as the familiar intro to Dad's favorite Earth, Wind & Fire song, "Devotion," played from the speakers.

"Let's go." Demi tugged me toward the kitchen. "Time to distract Pops from the letdown."

As we rounded the corner into the kitchen, Dad entered from the den and pulled Ma to him. They did a two-step while singing the lyrics to their song loudly. The rest of my siblings joined in, adding to the chorus. As everyone jumped into action, putting the finishing touches on the food, setting the table and pouring drinks, I realized that I missed this. I missed them. Even Duke. Because this was home. This was family. *My family*.

Soon, we were seated around the table, passing the food, talking about old times, and laughing at each other's expense. The doorbell rang right before Dad cut into the turkey.

Paityn stood. "That's probably my friend, Sasha."

She disappeared toward the front of the house. Seconds later, she was back and the woman standing with her was the same woman I'd seen outside of the bar and grill yesterday, the same woman who'd basically told me I wasn't shit. Grinning, Paityn introduced her friend to the family, starting with Dad. But when she got to Duke ...

"Nice to meet you," my brother said, shaking Sasha's hand.

Interesting.

Paityn squeezed my shoulders. "And this is my big brother, Tristan."

Sasha's eyes widened just a little bit before she steeled her expression, holding out her palm for me to grab it. "Nice to meet you, Tristan."

But I wasn't playing this game with her. "Still think I'm desperate?"

She didn't shy away from me either. "Maybe not."

Paityn's gaze flitted between me and Sasha. "You know each other?"

"I saw her yesterday. At Bar Louie." I met Duke's eyes, but my brother didn't react. "She was sitting at the bar alone, and I tried to talk to her." Demi tensed next to me, but I charged ahead anyway. "I offered to buy her a drink, but she turned me down cold. Called me desperate."

"You were a stranger to me," Sasha countered. "But next time we run into each other, you're more than welcome to buy me a drink."

Blake snickered. "It might be too late for that, Sasha. Mr. Fun Killer is cheap. He wouldn't even buy me a bomb pop from the ice cream truck."

Bliss cracked up. "I remember that. And you never forgave him, Sissy."

"Never," Blake agreed.

Demi excused herself, and I knew I'd fucked up. Again. Because I was incapable of letting shit rest. I couldn't go with Sasha's obvious plan to act like we'd never seen each other. Just like I couldn't let the night end without letting Duke know that I'd seen *him* without even saying the words.

I'm an asshole.

When Dallas stood to go after Demi, Duke placed his hand on hers. "It's okay." He glared at me. "I got this." Then he followed Demi to wherever she'd gone.

This muthafucka.

As my siblings took turns telling stories about my inability to have fun or spend my money, Sasha took her seat next to Paityn. Other than Dad, who pinned me with his patented you-ain't-slick look, the rest of the table didn't seem to recognize what had just transpired. Which was good.

35

Minutes later, Demi rejoined the table with Duke and sat down next to me. I attempted to squeeze her hand under the table, but she smacked my palm away. As I ate my pot roast in silence, I deliberated my next steps. Could I risk everything and be with Demi? Or …

I glanced up in time to catch Sasha peering at me curiously. *Nah, maybe I need to handle something else first?*

Chapter Three

TO DICK OR NOT TO DICK

Tristan

The Day After Thanksgiving, Many Years Ago

"*Y*ou ain't shit, Tristan!"

I still remembered the look in Blake's five-year-old eyes when she'd screamed it at the top of her lungs. After saving up for weeks, she'd dumped her entire bank in Ma's Cussing Jar just to be able to tell me that. All because I refused to buy her a popsicle on a hot summer day. Her words had stayed with me for years, too. Partly because it pissed me the fuck off. Mostly because she probably was right. Even now, I still suspected she felt that way. She wasn't the only one, though. And I knew it.

"Tristan, is everything okay?"

Demi's voice pulled me from my thoughts. From the moment I'd picked her up at my parents' house that morning, I knew I'd fucked up. Not because I didn't *want* to be there with her, but because I knew that I wasn't *ready* to be there with her. Now, I was almost frozen in indecision, torn between starting my car and driving us to the restaurant and admitting that this wasn't a good idea.

Turning to her, I sighed. "I'm sorry."

The apology hung in the air like a dark cloud ready to drench us both with an intense storm. It was the truth, though. I *was* sorry. For not giving her what I knew she needed from me. For hurting her every time I made unspoken promises that I couldn't fulfill. For not being good enough for her. Most of all, I was sorry I couldn't let her go—even though I knew I should.

A confused frown creased her forehead, but it disappeared quickly. She shifted in her seat, meeting my gaze. As she searched my eyes, her shoulders fell when realization dawned on her. "We're not going to breakfast, are we?"

I picked up her hand and kissed her palm. "Not today."

Demi blew out a slow breath. "I guess I should be glad you showed up this time to tell me in person."

"It's not you. And it's not forever. I need to get my shit together. There's a lot going on." That lie was wrapped in a blanket of truth. I absolutely had a lot on my plate. Nothing important enough to keep me away from her, though. No other women. No jobs. No appointments. *No excuses.*

"Didn't we go over this already?" she asked. "I don't need you to be perfect."

I placed her palm over my heart. "But *I* need to be perfect for you."

She eyed me skeptically. "I don't know what to say to that. I care about you so much, and I want to believe you, but it just sounds like bullshit to me."

"Do you believe I care about you?"

A tear fell from her eye, and I brushed it away with my thumb. "I want to," she whispered.

"Please believe me."

"Why should I?"

"Because I wouldn't be okay if you didn't," I confessed. "I know I don't have the right to ask you, but can you please give me some time? For now." Cupping her cheek in my palm, I continued, "You've been amazing to me. Your letters, the gifts … They kept me sane when I was away. I missed you."

"Really?" She pushed my hand away from her, folding her arms over her chest. "How was I supposed to know that? You never wrote back. And the one time you actually called—drunk off your ass—you told me you loved me. Then, I didn't hear from you again until last week when you invited me out and left me sitting alone in a restaurant waiting for you." She snickered. "I saw you that morning. Outside. I watched you walk away without a word."

I averted my gaze as a wave of guilt passed over me. "I'm sorry." The words felt hollow to my own ears, but I repeated myself two more times as if just saying it over and again would make it less fucked up.

"Don't. Stop apologizing. It's not going to change anything. Your words are not going to magically transport us back in time before you broke my heart."

"I don't want you to hate me. I'm—"

"Sorry?" She snickered. "Do you expect me to wait for you, to purposely avoid a meaningful relationship with anyone else on the oft chance that you get your shit together and come for me?"

I let out a heavy sigh. Demi had worked hard all her life to succeed. Despite her fucked-up parents, she'd excelled in school, graduated from college with honors, and promptly enrolled in law school at University of Michigan. Even at her age, she was a force to be reckoned with. And I wanted her to continue to soar. With or without me. "No, I want you to live your life."

"So you can come back and blow my shit up again?"

"I wouldn't do that to you."

Demi glared at me. "You already did." Her chin trembled as her expression softened. "The crazy part is I still can't turn my back on you. You're family regardless." She brushed her hand over my jaw, leaned forward, and kissed my cheek. "I love you, Tristan. I really do hope you figure your shit out like you want. But … this is where I get off the ride." She cast one last glance at me before she got out of my car and walked away from me.

I let her walk away, because deep down I knew that we were far from over. And if I played my cards right, she would let me back in. Because Demi had a heart of gold, and I was the greedy asshole who wanted the treasure at the end of the rainbow.

Several minutes later, I was still sitting outside in my car replaying that conversation over again when I heard a knock on the passenger window. After glancing over, I unlocked the door.

My little brother jumped in. "Can you drive me to the store?"

"No."

"Man, Tristan. Why?" Asa was a sophomore in high school, Ma's surprise to Dad after she'd sworn she was done having kids. "You know I don't have my license yet."

"And? What does that have to do with me?"

"I'm trying to get this new game console on a Black Friday deal."

Being the oldest of eight, I'd taken my responsibilities as big brother seriously. While Paityn nurtured them, I'd deemed myself as the disciplinarian. I didn't let them get away with shit, especially when their actions could hurt them physically or mentally. As a result, I was the "fun killer." The nickname had followed me into adulthood, but it didn't bother me at that time because it meant I was doing my job.

It wasn't until later that everything changed, and that innocent moniker became a noose around my neck. Because the knowledge that I was Sheila's son had stolen all my fun. Once everything clicked, all my shortcomings became magnified. I was the boy who wasn't like everyone else, the delinquent who would never fit in. I lashed out, pushed everyone away, and embraced the unexplainable anger that had always simmered beneath the surface. It was my defense mechanism against anyone who tried me, even my siblings. It was also my downfall because it left my relationships shattered. But of all my siblings, Asa still looked up to me.

"Duke was supposed to take me," Asa continued, "but he left this morning."

Curious, I asked Asa where Duke had gone. "Did he go to work? School?"

"I don't know. Somewhere. Overseas, I think."

My mind raced back to the conversation I had with Demi yesterday about Duke. "Is he good?"

"I don't know shit. I'm just here. They tell me nothing."

It was something we had in common, but I sensed my little brother was holding back. "But you know something?"

"A little." The reason he always knew "a little" was because people sometimes forgot he was in the room or because people assumed he wasn't listening. The truth was, Asa was an ear hustler. He knew a lot of secrets and only used them when the time was right for him.

"Well?" I prodded.

Asa sighed. "I heard he got into some trouble. Lost a lot of money. Flunked out of medical school. Tried to get out of it and ended up falling into a relationship with some old lady named Carolyn."

"So you know a lot."

Shrugging, he smirked. "Maybe. But I'm not saying anything else. I caught the way you were looking at Paityn's friend last night. You asked her out? Weren't you just with Demi?" Asa's ability to ask too many damn questions was on brand for the family. My parents were masters at badgering witnesses and pulling confessions out of reluctant informants. "Just wondering because she stormed in the house and slammed her bedroom door. She's pissed."

Another pang of guilt washed over me at the thought of Demi. "You ask too many questions, baby brotha."

He shrugged. "Isn't that how you get answers?"

"Do me a favor?"

Asa glanced at me. "What?"

"Keep an eye on her for me."

Frowning, he asked, "Why? Aren't you home for good now? You told me you weren't re-enlisting. And you just started your business."

"Who told you that?"

"I think Paityn. Or I heard Ma and Dad talking about it. What kind of business is it?"

"Private investigator." My cellphone buzzed, and I glanced down at the screen. *Britt.* I sent the call to voicemail fully knowing she wouldn't handle it well. I turned to

Asa, gave him some dap. "Now get yo' ass out my damn car. I got shit to do."

He shook his head. "There you go. I gave up the information. The least you could do is take me to GameStop. Damn."

I chuckled. "Check the backseat."

Asa shifted to do as he was told. "What the …?" He pulled the box off the seat. "You bought me a PS2?" He smiled, holding the game system in the air. "How did you know?"

"I just did." After dinner, I'd caught a glimpse of Ma's Christmas shopping list. Since I couldn't sleep last night, I got my ass up early and stood in that long line at the store to pick it up. While I didn't usually buy gifts for my siblings, I'd been away for a while and would more than likely miss Asa's birthday party in a couple of weeks. "Happy Birthday and Merry Christmas. Now, go."

Asa bumped my fist with his. "Thanks, bruh. I'm 'bout to be on this bad boy all day."

Once he sprinted into the house, I called Britt back. "What's up?"

"Can you meet me at the hotel?" Britt said, skipping the pleasantries.

"Nah." As much as my dick liked her pussy, the fact that she'd threatened my balls made my decision to end this thing between us. "I think it's time we cool it."

"Nigga, please. Dick is free in the hood, and I don't need *yours* to get what I want. I do need your *business* expertise, though. Have you thought about my offer?"

My dick twitched, probably because that muthafucka liked a challenge. "I'm gon' have to pass on that, too." The money would be good for my life and my business, but Britt wasn't. It was obvious she was into some crazy shit, and I wanted no part of it. "It's not for me right now."

"Shit," she hissed. "What if I double your fee?"

"Tempting, but no."

"Do you know anyone with your particular skillset that could be of assistance?"

There were several people who'd gladly take her job, but I only gave her one name. "Stone Cross."

"Is that his real name?" she asked.

Instead of answering her question, I simply gave her his contact information. "Tell him I sent you."

"Thank you. One more thing."

"Yes?"

"I shouldn't have to tell you this, but can I count on you to keep our interaction quiet?"

"Of course," I assured her. We didn't waste any more time on pleasantries. I told her, "Take care," then ended the call.

I really wasn't shit.

And what I was about to do was fucked up. But even though I realized I could've chosen to do anything other than what I was currently doing, I still forged ahead. I hopped out of my car and walked toward my destination.

The apartment community was quiet from what I'd seen during my hours-long surveillance. Obviously, the owners took great care of their property. The grass was cut, the walks were shoveled. There was no trash on the concrete. No bums or troublemakers lingering in the parking lot or the courtyard where the playground was situated. No loud music blasting from cars. No vicious arguments on site. The tenants I'd observed included several older couples, a single mother of two elementary-aged kids, and a few college students. Everyone seemed to get along, often stopping to chat with their neighbors as they entered or exited the building.

As I approached apartment 5405, I spotted a woman entering the front door, so I hung back. She appeared to be pregnant, maybe six months or so. *That* did give me pause, and for the first time since I'd arrived, I considered turning back. The door swung open again, and the same woman emerged and hurried back to the apartment next door. I made a mental note to find out how she was connected to this.

Stepping up to the door, I brought my hand up to knock, but the door opened before my fist could connect with the hard wood. Sasha's smile fell instantly. Eyes wide, she stepped outside of the apartment, closing the door behind her.

With narrowed eyes, she assessed me. "What the hell are you doing here?" she asked through clenched teeth. "Are you following me?"

"What do you do when desperation comes knocking at your door?"

She folded her arms over her chest. It was the first time I noticed a baby cup in her hand. "One of two things— stand my ground or call the police. Which do you prefer?"

She's feisty. I lifted my hands up in surrender. "Neither."

"I can't believe this. Paityn is well adjusted. Her parents are phenomenal. Mr. Young wrote me a glowing recommendation for a teaching assistant job. Then, there's you."

I barked out a laugh, caught off guard by her candor. "Wow."

"I'm not laughing. What the hell do you want?"

"What about Duke?" I asked. "Is *he* well adjusted?"

She shrugged. "Obviously, I caught the way you taunted your brother by telling him you met me at Bar Louie. You already know I know him, so I'm not going to deny it. I'm also not going to tell you anything about my dealings with Duke because it's none of your business."

She's also bold, unafraid. "My siblings are my business," I told her.

"Is that why you're here now? Concern for Duke?"

"Maybe."

"That's laughable. It's clear to me that you and Duke have some sort of *thing* with each other. It was on full display at dinner. And I'm going to say this one time— leave me out of that shit."

And she's sharp. "Fine. I can admit that I took this too far."

With a raised brow, she asked, "Why?"

"Honestly?"

"No." The sarcasm dripped from her tone. "I actually want you to lie after you came all this way to see me."

I paused. There were many things I could say, but I felt like my best option was the truth. "You're right. I came here because I saw you with Duke," I admitted. "I was curious when you pretended not to know him at Thanksgiving dinner."

Sasha searched my eyes. "So you chose to come to my apartment?"

I opened my mouth to speak, but …

I got nothing.

"Tristan?"

"I'm a private investigator," I offered lamely. "I always want to make sure my family is good. Even Duke." Her shoulders fell, so I took that opportunity to add, "And because I wanted to take you out for a drink."

"You do realize this is crazy, right?"

"You called it. I'm desperate," I joked.

A smirk pulled at her full lips. "You're a private investigator, huh?"

"I am."

"What else do you do?"

I pinned her with my gaze. "Whatever you need."

The door swung open behind her, and an older woman poked her head out. "Sasha?" She glanced at me, concern in her eyes. "Are you okay?"

From inside of the apartment, I heard Elmo. I knew the voice because Raven had carried her Tickle Me Elmo doll around everywhere for a period. Turning to the lady, Sasha smiled. "I'm fine, Ola." She handed her the cup. "I'll be in soon."

A little girl toddled to the door and somehow dodged the older woman's grasp to get to Sasha. She lifted her arms in the universal sign to pick her up. "Ma Ma."

This was a new development, one that I hadn't anticipated because I'd only done a quick internet search on her. Sasha didn't have a MySpace or Facebook page, but Paityn did. I found out she was employed at Bar Louie because my sister had posted a picture of the two of them with the caption "Ran into my friend, who treated me to the best margarita I've ever tasted."

While my actions today may have indicated that I was *that* guy, I really wasn't. And other than her address, her employer, an old news article highlighting her accomplishments in high school, and the little tidbits I learned from eavesdropping on her conversation with my family on Thanksgiving, I didn't know much about her. I'd purposely chosen *not* to do a full background check because, after I met her, invading her privacy didn't quite sit right.

Sasha picked her baby girl up, kissing her brow. Then, she handed her to Ola. "Please, take her inside."

The woman eyed me skeptically. "I'm here if you need me."

"It's okay, Ma. I got this."

I knew the older woman wasn't her mother thanks to Bliss. When the women were talking at the house, Bliss had asked about her mother and Sasha was upfront about her loss. I kept that to myself, though. I also decided not to mention anything to her about the woman I saw leaving her apartment earlier.

Ola glared at me one more time before she took the baby inside and closed the door.

"How old is she?" I asked.

"You don't know already? I'm assuming you know where I live because you investigated me."

I shook my head as shame rolled over me. "No. Actually, I didn't do much." The fact that she'd never answered my question didn't escape me and I decided not to push.

"Paityn doesn't know," she confessed.

I wasn't surprised. In fact, I was convinced my sister didn't know much about her friend. And I suspected Sasha preferred it that way. "Does Paityn know anything about you?"

"She knows that I'm a grad student at University of Michigan. She knows that I deferred college to work because my scholarships didn't really cover my tuition. She knows that I'm nothing like her. She's not bothered that I'm closed off, that I don't feel comfortable disclosing personal information about myself or my past. Yet, she's been kind to me even though others have been rude and condescending."

"That sounds like my sister."

"I appreciate her. And I would appreciate it if you kept this quiet."

"You don't have to worry. I won't say anything."

She stared at me, studied me with those brown eyes. "I don't, do I?"

"I like to keep things quiet myself. But, if I wanted to

share a secret, I'd tell Paityn." I didn't know why, but I sensed Sasha needed a real friend. Someone she could be herself with, someone she could trust. And my sister was one of the best people I knew. "She's good at keeping people's confidence."

"Thanks for the advice."

"Anytime."

We stood there in silence for a moment. "One drink," she offered. "Are you available next Friday?"

No. But plans were made to be canceled. "Yes. I can pick you up at six—"

"Meet me at *seven* o'clock. At Bar Louie." She opened her door and stepped inside. "Never come back here again. Don't think that being Paityn's brother will stop me from protecting my space."

Then she slammed the door.

Chapter Four

OTHER SIDE OF THE GAME

Sasha

December, Many Years Ago

I pretended to study while Ola stared at me from across the room. I'd managed to avoid her questions about our unwelcome visitor this afternoon, but I knew she wouldn't accept my silence much longer.

I shot her a sidelong glance, then let my gaze fall on my sleeping daughter. I knew what Ola was thinking. We'd come so far, and I didn't have time to be distracted by a fine-ass man with baggage. Because, yes, I could look at Tristan and see that he was a lot. There was a darkness in his eyes that should scare any woman who dared to get involved with him in any way. Still, I wasn't opposed to exploiting his particular skillset to get what I needed. If that meant I needed to have a drink or two with him to meet my goal, I would do it in a heartbeat. The fact that he was Paityn's brother almost made it okay to trust him. *Just a little bit.* And just for a purpose.

"I don't trust him," Ola announced as she stacked a pile of magazines on the coffee table.

I shrugged. "I understand. But I'm not marrying the guy. We're just having a drink."

"It always starts with a drink. Next thing you know, he's moving in."

"Since when?" I challenged. "I've only ever lived with one man in my life."

She waved a dismissive hand my way. "Not you, chile. Just … I know the type. Smooth. Dark. And trouble."

I closed my eyes and sucked in a deep breath. "Ola, he's not Trevor. And I'm not you. Sometimes we let our past control our future. Then, we end up missing something beneficial to our big picture. Tristan has connections. If I remember correctly, he just got out of the military. He owns a business. And he's a rule breaker."

Ola snickered. "I know he didn't tell you all of that?"

"No, he didn't."

"So how do you know that we can trust him?" she challenged.

"Because Paityn Young is an honest, trustworthy person. Tristan is her brother."

"And? My brother is crazy as hell. And your brothers —" She swallowed. "I'm sorry, Sasha."

The subject of my brothers always came with grief for several reasons. We lost our mother at a very young age, and my oldest brother Nero had to go live with his deceased father's parents. He was the lucky one. His grandparents were pillars in the community and ensured that he remained on solid footing. He had support. Me and the rest of my siblings … Well, we had *my* father.

The day of my mother's funeral, my dad picked us up, drove us away from everything we knew, and dumped us at his mother's house. Granny worked day and night until she died, then we basically raised ourselves. The only time Dad showed up was when the social security survivor's check came.

We had vowed to do better, to succeed where our parents failed. Except, we had little support. No money. Shit, we barely had food to eat. And my older brother, Shaun, had taken it upon himself to make sure we were fed. Which meant he'd done some street shit to survive. And now he was dead. My other brother, Vincent, left Michigan for parts unknown as soon as he turned eighteen.

"It's fine," I grumbled.

Ola took the empty seat next to me and held my hand. "No, really. I miss him, too."

When my grandmother died, Ola tried to help us as much a she could. She was the school nurse and had risked her own job to make sure we had what we needed, even going so far as to petition the court for legal guardianship of us. But my father made sure she wasn't successful, and unfortunately, the court believed him when he said he was an active, present father in our lives. He'd even filed a complaint against Ola for trespassing when she'd drop off food and supplies.

"I think about what things would be like today if he was here," she added.

"Maybe they'd be worse?" I suggested. As much as I loved Shaun, his life was full of drama and danger. I definitely wouldn't be comfortable having him around Ashlyn.

But I *did* miss him, and I hated the fact that he never had the chance to meet my daughter because he was killed the month before I gave birth.

"Don't say that," Ola chastised.

Ash stirred and let out a cute cry before settling back to sleep. I stared at my daughter. My life was one of questionable choices, dangerous risks. But I'd always been smart enough to know that my only way out of the hood was through either hard work or luck. I chose to go to college, to get my degree. And now I was enrolled in graduate school, because I needed to be able to provide a good life for her. She was my reason to leave my past behind. She was my reason for everything.

"Sasha?"

Ola's voice pulled me from my thoughts, and I met her concerned stare. "Have you heard from Josslyn?" I asked, changing the subject. I hadn't heard from my sister in a few weeks. Which was unusual for her.

"Leah said she called this morning while I was at the grocery store," Ola explained.

The door swung open, and my sister-in-law, Leah, entered the apartment. "Dinner is ready."

Leah was my late brother's wife. She'd been part of my life since we were teenagers, and I considered her family. Before Shaun died, they had struggled to conceive, and had started the in vitro process. Although his death was hard on her, she'd made the decision to go forth with their plan and now she was pregnant with my nephew.

I smiled at her. "You're so cute with the waddle."

Laughing, Leah sat down on the couch. "Don't remind me. I can't wait for these cankles to go away." She yawned. "I'm exhausted just from that little walk over here."

When I decided to attend graduate school in Ann

Arbor, I chose to move to a suburb of Detroit, Dearborn, Michigan. I rented two apartments, one for me and one for Leah because I'd promised Shaun that I would always look out for her. And when Ola fell on hard times, I moved her in with me. Having her there had been invaluable, and she took good care of Ashlyn while I worked. I loved our little community and wanted to expand it. Once I graduated and set up my practice, I planned to purchase land and build homes for women who were displaced whether it was through an abusive relationship or other circumstances beyond their control.

Leah glanced at me, then Ola. "Did I miss something?"

Ola pointed at me. "This one here had some random man stop by unannounced."

Rolling my eyes, I explained, "He wasn't 'some random man,' Ola. I told you his name and who he's related to."

Grinning, Leah arched a brow. "Who is he? Someone you're dating?"

"I don't date. You know that."

"Okay, is he someone you're fucking?" Leah asked.

Ola's mouth fell open. "Leah!"

"What?" Leah shrugged. "You know our girl hasn't been fucked in years. I, for one, will be happy when she finds her a nice man and sits on his dick."

I cracked up. "Sis!"

Ola covered her smile. "Shhh. Little ears, Leah."

"She's two." Leah never had a problem speaking her mind. That mouth got her in trouble many times, but she didn't care. She reminded me of who I used to be, before my life took a drastic turn. "She doesn't know the difference between blue and green. She damn sure doesn't know what a penis is."

"Your language, Leah," Ola pressed. "You're going to be a mother soon. It's time to tone it down."

Leah sucked her teeth. "Ma, I love you. I really do. But the world is different now than it was when you were young."

"How old do you think I am, Leah?" Ola asked incredulously.

I giggled at the mortified expression on Ola's face. She hated being associated with her age group, even if it was the truth. We called her Ma because she acted *and* dressed motherly. "It doesn't matter. You're you. And you've been such a Godsend in our lives. Right, Leah?" I eyed Leah expectantly, praying that she would just drop it.

Leah didn't look convinced. The two of them were like oil and water. They argued constantly. I suspected it had a lot to do with how alike Ola and Leah's estranged mother were. "Right," she grumbled.

"To answer your question, though," I said, "Tristan is my friend Paityn's brother."

Leah nodded. "Okay. I remember Paityn." I'd introduced to two of them about a month ago. "She's a sweetie."

"I know, right?" I agreed. "I met her brother at Bar Louie, and he asked me out. At the time, I didn't know who he was, but we met officially at her house on Thanksgiving."

"You mean when you left us to fend for ourselves to eat good food with the rich family?"

The argument that ensued once I told Ola and Leah about my plans had been one for the books, especially when I decided to leave Ashlyn at home with them. "I'm not getting into this again. Stop acting like I deserted you. We had a full dinner here first, and I was only gone for a couple of hours."

"Whatever." Leah stood. "Dinner's getting cold."

With my busy schedule, I rarely cooked. Ola and Leah took turns making sure we all ate. I checked my watch. "I can't stay. I have to take care of something."

Ola frowned. "What is it?"

"Business." My stomach fell when I noticed the worried glances they exchanged. I couldn't blame them, though. Up until recently, my nightly excursions could've landed me in trouble. "It's not what you think," I added. "I'll be back before nine."

"Can I ask where you're going?" Leah asked. I expected that question to come from Ola, but Ma was quiet as a mouse as she folded clothes.

"To see Carolyn."

Ola lifted her gaze, but still didn't speak.

Leah nibbled on her bottom lip. "Are you sure about this?"

"I need to check on her." I tugged my coat on and smiled, rubbing Leah's belly. "Save me a plate?"

"I will. But you better be careful."

"You know I will." I stopped in front of Ola on my way to the door and waited for her to look at me again. "Remember when you told me that we should always look out for people who are struggling?"

Ola swallowed visibly. "I find it hard to believe that *she's* struggling."

I squeezed her hand. "Trust me, she is. And I have to be there for her. Because if it wasn't for her, we wouldn't be here. The tuition wouldn't be paid. Leah wouldn't be pregnant with my nephew. Our rent would be due, and *he* would've made mine and Ashlyn's life a living hell."

I didn't have to say his name for them to know who I was talking about. They knew better than most what I suffered through longer than I cared to admit. Because if it wasn't for Carolyn, and my daughter's father was still around, there would be nowhere I could hide.

Gripping the steering wheel, I took several deep breaths before I exited my trusty yet old Pontiac Grand-Am. I stared up at the non-descript bungalow and thought about how quickly life could change. Not even two months ago, Carolyn lived in a spacious mansion outside of Detroit. Now, she was holed up in a rental property on the West Side of Detroit.

I scanned the area before making my way up the front door. Once I knocked, I spun around and stared up and down the street. I'd learned a long time ago never to turn my back on the block. One distraction could be the difference between life and death. The door opened behind me, and I turned slightly.

Carolyn smiled sadly, then opened the door for me. Once I stepped inside, I followed her through the living room toward the back of the house. She poured us a cup of tea and brought both mugs over to the kitchen table. I took that as my cue to have a seat.

We sat in silence for several minutes, but it wasn't uncomfortable. I'd studied the human mind extensively, but most of my skills were learned by experience, from interacting with people, from watching cues. As I sipped my tea, I allowed myself the opportunity to look around the kitchen. There wasn't much to it. Nothing fancy like the kitchen I'd spent so much time in before. A small stove, microwave, an apartment-size refrigerator, and minimal cabinet space. There was no island, no wine cooler, no convection ovens, no stainless-steel appliances.

"This is temporary," she muttered, turning her mug in her palm.

When she met my gaze, I gasped at the hollow look in her eyes. Carolyn used to be the life of any party. Her hair was always styled perfectly. Her makeup, flawless. Her eyes bright. And her smile was contagious. Tonight, she seemed like an imposter. Definitely not the woman I'd known for so long. The woman who could command a room, instill fear in the biggest thugs in the city. "I'll be back on top shortly. My lawyers have assured me."

I nodded. "I believe that." The alternative wasn't something I wanted to imagine.

I met her when I was bartending at a hotel downtown. She'd entered with an entourage, countless people ready to jump for her. To the world, she was the owner of one of the largest HR consulting firms in the country—The Fuller Group. Behind the scenes, she commanded a high-class escort service. Because of that, she had more power than the Mayor of Detroit and she knew how to use it. Carolyn Fuller was the master of pulling strings. She kept her clients' secrets, and they kept her rich.

The first time she noticed me, she commented on my dull lipstick and lopsided ponytail. I could still remember the way she'd looked me up and down, almost with disdain. But there was a curiosity there, too. Then, she slid a crisp hundred-dollar bill across the bar top and ordered me to take it and get my hair done.

When the manager of the bar broke his neck to greet her, she ordered him to assign me to her private party that night. I made over five thousand dollars in tips in less than four hours. Our next conversation occurred the following day when she offered me a job.

I was young, but I wasn't naïve. While I served drinks, I'd noticed how the men perused the young women in the room. I'd seen several transactions between interested parties. And I didn't want any part of it, so I turned her down. She laughed in my face, then told me I didn't have what it took to work for her in *that* way.

"I can tell you're smart. I don't want you to date the men. I need you to be my eyes in the room."

Intrigued, I'd visited her at her home. I met her husband and her daughter. She put me at ease, assuring me that I would never have to sleep with any man to make a buck. That day, I accepted her offer and joined her company as her hostess-slash-personal assistant.

"Can I help you in any way?" I asked finally.

She chuckled. "At least you didn't ask how I was doing."

The low rasp in her throat was comforting. I always knew that when she was in a room, I was going to be taken care of.

I grabbed her hands and squeezed. "I can come here and sit with you. Clean. Cook. Anything."

Carolyn offered me another sad smile. "No. I don't want you anywhere near me. I hate that you came here because I can't risk you getting pulled into this."

Over the last few months, Carolyn's empire had collapsed under the weight of her indiscretions. The scandal of her affair with Duke Young ruined her marriage and destroyed her livelihood. Her husband had one mission—revenge. Every week, he filed a new motion. The dominoes continued to fall, and yesterday, an anonymous source leaked documents exposing her as the head of the escort company, basically opening her up for criminal charges.

"I'm worried," I confessed. "Now that it's out—"

"No one's going to touch me," she said. "You should know by now that I'm never down or out. This place may be small, but I'm fine here, baby. There are people placed all around this block, ready and willing to protect me."

I let out a breathless chuckle. "I should've known."

"But you can't come back here."

"I just had to see you. I don't know where I would be without you."

"You'd be fine."

I shook my head. "I wouldn't. You saved my life."

"Call us even. Your eyes in the room saved *my* life many times."

"Thank you for everything."

"Just take care of yourself and your beautiful baby. There's nothing holding you back from following your dreams." She got up and disappeared around the corner, then returned a few minutes later with a white envelope. Holding it up, she said, "This is for you. Consider it your severance package."

I pushed the envelope back at her. "No, you need to keep this. I know he froze your accounts."

She smirked. "You do know who I am, right? I got it."

Finally, I took the envelope, but didn't count the contents. Standing, I gave her a quick hug. "You know where to reach me."

Carolyn nodded. "If anyone comes to you, threatens you, or—"

"I know how to take care of myself," I assured her.

"I don't doubt that, but I need you to tell me. I can get someone over there to watch over you and your people."

"I'm good," I whispered as tears burned my throat. "I promise."

"You should go."

As we walked to the front door, I thought about everything I wanted to say to her, but nothing would come out. Before I turned the knob, I turned to her. "I'll be in touch."

"Only if it's an emergency," she corrected.

"Got it. I've never told you this before, but I love you."

Her expression softened as tears filled her eyes and spilled down her cheeks. It was the first time I'd ever seen her cry. "Baby, you need to go."

I brushed the moisture from her face. "Right."

As I hurried to my car, I could've sworn I heard her call me, but when I turned back, the door was closed, and the house was dark.

Chapter Five

THIS IS

Sasha

December, Many Years Ago

"*L*ook at my baby!" I blew into Ashlyn's stomach and cracked up when she dissolved into giggles. "I love you." I kissed her belly. "I love you." I kissed her forehead. "I love you." I lifted her into my arms and twirled around.

"Aw." Ola crossed her arms over her chest as she watched me play with my baby. "I love to see you happy."

Bouncing Ash in my arms, I danced across the floor with her. "I love these moments."

"Josslyn called," Ola announced.

I made a face at Ash. "Did she? Is she good?"

"I guess," Ola replied, biting down on her lip.

My smile faltered. "What do you mean?"

My younger sister, Josslyn, had struggled for years with depression and anxiety. None of us had come away unscathed from our childhood, but I had hoped Joss was on an upward trajectory when she landed a coveted internship in her field last summer, followed by an amazing job offer at the same company. She was in her last year of undergrad at Michigan State University and was due to graduate next spring.

"Does she need anything?" I asked.

"She said she's good on money. But she didn't sound right."

I set Ashlyn into her highchair and went into the kitchen to fix her dinner. "Maybe I should pop up on her."

"She specifically asked us not to do that."

"I'll call her."

A knock pulled our attention to the door. "Can you finish this?" I asked.

Frowning, Ola said, "Are you expecting someone?"

"Yes."

I shuffled to the door and peered through the peephole. Taking a deep breath, I opened the door. "Hi!"

Paityn grinned. "Hey." She held up a bottle of wine. "I brought wine. For later."

I took the offered gift. "Thanks. Come in."

She stepped into my apartment. "I wasn't sure if I should bring food?"

"Are you hungry?" I asked, shifting from one foot to the other.

Now that she was there, in my space, I couldn't help but rethink my decision to invite her over to study. It was the first time I invited anyone to my apartment. Tristan's words haunted me for the entire week. Because he was right. I did need a friend. Someone other than Ola and

Leah to talk to, to trust. I sent up a silent prayer that Paityn was indeed that person for me.

I took her coat. "We already ate, but there's plenty left."

She giggled when her stomach growled. "You said the magic word. I'm starved."

"You can set your bag down," I told her. "I'll make you a plate."

Paityn looked around as she followed me to the kitchen. "I love your place." She stopped at the wall, where an abstract of Street Life hung on the wall—my first purchase for the apartment. "This is beautiful." She stared up at the painting. "Did you do this?"

I snickered. "No, girl. I'm many things, but creative is not one of them."

She laughed. "My sister would love it. She dabbles."

"Which sister?"

"Bliss," she answered. "She drags us to art shows and museums every chance she gets."

"Ah, I love it. One of the first things I did when I moved back to Detroit was purchase a membership at the DIA."

The Detroit Institute of Art Museum was one of my favorite places in the city. I made it a point to go to exhibitions whenever I could. Even if there was nothing planned, I often went just to browse the collections.

"That's cool." Paityn tore her gaze away from the painting and glanced at me. "You should really hook up with Bliss. She has a membership there, too."

"Good to know."

I held my breath as I rounded the corner. Ola met my gaze with surprised eyes. "Ma, this is my friend, Paityn."

Ola blinked but held out her hand. "Hi. I'm Ola."

Paityn shook her hand. "Hello."

"Ola is a good friend of my family," I explained. "Like a mother to me and my siblings."

"Nice to meet you, Ola." Her gaze fell to Ashlyn who was now wearing her dinner on her face. "And who is this?" She picked up a napkin and wiped some sweet potato from Ash's nose. "Aren't you just a cutie pie?" she said in a baby voice. "So pretty."

My eyes landed on Ola. Then on Paityn. And finally on my baby girl. I smiled. "Paityn, this is my daughter."

Paityn's eyes widened, but she recovered quickly. "Oh. I had no idea you were a mom. She's so beautiful. How old is she?"

"Two. Since you so graciously opened your home to me for the holiday, I figured it was time to introduce you to my world."

Eyeing me curiously, Paityn said, "Thank you for trusting me with this." She searched my face, almost like she was peeling back my layers, like she was seeing me for the first time. "It wasn't easy for you, was it?"

I let out a nervous giggle. "No."

She squeezed my hand. "Your secret is safe with me."

I sighed with relief because I didn't even tell her to keep the secret. She just knew. "Thank you."

"Can I hold her?"

"Sure."

Paityn played with Ashlyn while I fixed her plate. We chatted while she ate. I learned that Paityn wanted a big family, but definitely not as many kids as her mother had. She talked about her siblings, and even inadvertently gave me some information on Tristan that I felt would come in handy when we met tomorrow night for drinks. Once she finished her food, Ola offered to bathe Ashlyn so that we could study.

I cleared the table. "I really appreciate you coming

over, especially since you live so far." She lived about forty miles away, in Ann Arbor. "Maybe we should get started so you won't have to drive home too late."

Paityn waved a dismissive hand my way. "Girl, please. I don't mind the drive."

When I joined her at the table, she stared at me. "What?" I asked.

"Did you really want to study tonight?"

I scratched the back of my neck. "Not really."

She cracked up, closing her notebook. "I didn't think so."

Leaning forward, I rested my elbows on the table. "This is going to sound so crazy, but I really just needed a friend."

"It's not crazy." She placed a hand on top of mind. "I need one, too."

"You're so close to your sisters, though."

"That's why I need a friend," she muttered. "Shoot, you met them."

I chuckled. "They are hilarious."

"I hope you don't mind me asking, but is Ashlyn's father in the picture?"

A cold chill ran down my spine. "No. He died a little over a year ago."

Paityn's expression softened. "I'm sorry."

"I'm not." I didn't want to get into my past with my daughter's father, but I wanted to make it clear how I felt about him. "Trust me, we're better off with him gone."

She squeezed my hand, steadying my nerves. "You have a support system, so that's good."

"Leah lives next door. You met her a while ago."

"Right. How is she? If I remember correctly, she was very pregnant."

"She's taking it easy. I'm surprised she didn't show up

tonight. The walls are paper thin. I'm sure she heard the laughter."

Revealing pieces of myself wasn't easy for me, but I had no doubt that I'd made the right decision. As we talked about school, Paityn's love life, and my aversion to men with too much hair on their chest, I silently thanked God for answering my prayer.

———

Bar Louie was packed—people congregating at the bar, couples cuddling up together in booths, and large parties celebrating each other. When I arrived, I immediately regretted not being on the clock, because it was sure to be a good night for tips.

The hostess, Shauna, greeted me with a smile. "Hey, girl. I didn't know you were on the clock."

"I'm not." I slipped my coat off and scanned the room.

"You better not let Carlos see you," Shauna mentioned. "He's short-staffed at the bar."

I spotted Tristan sitting at a corner booth, on the far side of the restaurant. "Well, let me just walk my ass over to my table then before he sees me."

I said my goodbye and made my way to the table. Tristan's eyes met mine as I neared the booth and …

Damn. I knew he was hot, but … Shit. Like the other times I'd seen him, he was dressed in dark clothes. A button-down shirt and jeans. Simple but sexy. His head was freshly shaven, his beard groomed. Suddenly, Leah's suggestion that I take this opportunity to get fucked didn't seem so bad.

No, I chided myself as wayward thoughts threatened to overtake my common sense.

He stood. "Hey."

Oh, God, his voice. The raspy sound vibrated through my body. "Hey." I let out a shaky breath. "Sorry I'm late."

"Just glad you made it." He gestured for me to take the seat across from him and sat down once I was settled.

A gentleman, too. "What would you have done if I hadn't shown up?"

He shrugged. "Nothing."

I narrowed my eyes on him. "I can't say I believe you."

His tongue darted out to wet his lips, and I couldn't tear my eyes away from the motion. "I understand why you don't. I didn't make the best first impression."

"At least you can admit when you fucked up."

He chuckled. "You got me."

The waitress arrived to take our order. Once she left, I leaned forward. "So. Tell me why you asked me out. Really."

With a raised brow, he said, "Isn't that obvious?"

"I don't know. Is this your attempt to one-up Duke?"

"Do I have to?" he tossed back.

"No. There is nothing romantic going on between me and your brother."

He leaned forward. "Good to know."

I wasn't sure if it was the lighting or his cologne that made me feel warm. And a little reckless. "One more question."

"Okay."

"Demi?" She tapped her finger on the table. "There's something between you two?"

"Very observant."

"Occupational hazard."

"Which job is that?"

His comment gave me pause, and I wondered if he knew more than he was letting on. "I'm a bartender. I get paid to serve drinks and listen to people's problems."

"But you're also studying to be a therapist, right?"

"Right." Despite my obvious attraction to him, there was something about him that felt too intense. The last time I'd felt anything even remotely similar was when I met …

"You should know I will never come to your place again."

"Good to know," I said, mimicking his words from earlier.

"Unless you invite me," he added.

Warmth spread to my fingers and toes. *Maybe I just need a good vibrator.* "You don't have to worry about that," I quipped.

Tristan smirked. "You're funny."

"Strangely enough, no one has ever told me that before."

Growing up in my house, there wasn't much to laugh about. I'd taken on the role of caretaker for my siblings, even though I was the second youngest. I made sure clothes were washed, the house was cleaned, and dinner was cooked. I handled the household finances, which wasn't much, so I excelled at budgeting. Even at ten, I could balance an account.

"Something we have in common."

The waitress brought our drinks. "That doesn't surprise me." I took a sip and grimaced. Too much sour, not enough tequila. "I could tell at Thanksgiving. So serious."

"A lot going on that day."

Once again, I studied him. I'd always been interested in people—what they loved, what they hated, how they lived, how they loved. I could spend hours every day just watching strangers. Getting the chance to figure someone out excited me. And Tristan was now at the top of my list.

For tonight anyway. "Answer the question. Finally. You and Demi?"

"We're family."

His answer was safe. *And probably true.* While I didn't doubt they were *like* family, I sensed there was more between them. "And?"

"That's it. For now."

"Not because of her, though," I mused. "It's all you."

He eyed me over the rim of his glass. "It's always me."

I shifted in my seat as my stomach did an odd flip. "You're not a player."

"Nah," he confirmed. "That's not me."

"But you also aren't the type to settle down."

"Are you writing your thesis on me, Sasha?"

I grinned then. Pointing my fork at him, I said, "Did you just make a joke, Tristan?"

He barked out a laugh. "Maybe."

"Okay, so you and Demi?"

"You're not going to let this go, are you?"

Nope. I wasn't sure why either. I just had to know if what I sensed was real. "Just answer the question. Better yet … Does Demi think she's your girlfriend?"

He snickered. "No. Definitely not."

"Does Demi *want* to be your girlfriend?"

"Not anymore," he confessed.

"You hurt her." It wasn't a question because I already knew the answer.

"I did, and I regret that."

Swallowing, I picked up a napkin and folded the edges. "Can you fix it?"

"Not right now. One day, I hope."

"That's … honest." It still wasn't a complete answer to my question, but it was refreshing. To hear that he actually regretted the hurt he'd caused. And, God help me, it made him more attractive. *I need to get out of here*. We sat in silence for a moment. "As much as I'm enjoying asking all the questions, I have to go."

Tristan didn't move. "Okay."

"You're not going to say anything else?"

"Sasha?"

My eyes dropped to his mouth. "Huh?"

"I'm not in the habit of begging someone to stay. I do want to set the record straight, though."

Damn it, I couldn't stop looking at his mouth. "What is it?"

"You called me desperate. And I'm anything but …"

I nodded. "Point taken."

He set a business card on the table. "Last week, you seemed curious about my job. If you need something, call me." He scribbled an address on the back of the card. "I'm staying here for the time being."

I lifted my gaze. "Are you planning to leave soon?"

"Probably."

"Why are you being so nice?"

"Because I have a daughter to protect, too. I know the feeling."

I picked up the card and brushed my thumb over the embossing. "Good to know. Full disclosure, I did want to talk to you about a job, but I got distracted trying to trip you up with questions."

"I'm not surprised. Call me when you're ready."

"For what?" I croaked.

"Anything."

Tristan was definitely a problem. And if I wasn't careful, I'd be in trouble. So, my best course of action was to walk away. I pushed my still-full glass away and stood. "Thanks for the drink. I enjoyed myself."

"You're welcome."

Pivoting on my heels, I hurried out of the bar. Instead of going home, I decided to take a drive. It wasn't the safest decision, but I ended up at my old house. I didn't go there often, but I needed a reminder, a reset. Being there was a stark reminder of where I'd come from. Staring at the dark, abandoned home, I thought about everything that happened this year. The incredible strides I'd made and the devastating low moments. But none of that compared to the time I'd spent in that small, brick house. *With him.* A tear escaped as memories filled every space of my mind.

Despite the many setbacks I'd had, the dreams deferred, I was still there. Still kicking. Still fighting. Still surviving. And wouldn't let anyone or anything distract me from my goals.

Resolved, I drove away from the house, from the past once again. I didn't go home, though. Because …

Maybe I can afford a little detour? I knew what I had to do to ensure my daughter lived the life she deserved. But I also knew what I wanted at this very moment. I parked my car and placed a call.

"Ma? Hey. How's my baby?"

"She's good," Ola said. "We just turned on *Peppa Pig.*"

I smiled, picturing my girl's beautiful face. "Good. I'll be home in a little bit."

Once I ended the call, I checked my surroundings, and got out of the car. As I approached the door, I questioned whether I was doing the right thing. In the end, though, I decided to turn off the voices screaming at me to go home and knocked on the door.

It took a few seconds, but the door swung open. "Hi."

Tristan stared down at me. "Hi."

Then he let me in.

Chapter Six

WICKED GAMES

Tristan

*B*ack in the day, my mother would set up special dates with each of us. It was her way of giving us alone time with her. Sometimes we'd catch a movie. Other times, we'd have a picnic in the park. When I got older, the types of things we did together changed as Ma tailored each experience to fit the child she was with. I hated sitting still, so she scheduled outings that required movement—like skating or bowling, hiking or even rock climbing. My time with her usually ended with me doing whatever activity she'd signed us up for and her sitting on a bench and rooting for me.

Later, I realized she did that so we could feel close to her. She pushed herself aside, ignoring her fear of bugs so that she could be outside with me or pretending not to be scared of heights when we went rock climbing. When I asked her why she did it, she'd simply shrugged and said, "Because you love it. And I love you."

I couldn't receive the words at the time because I was in a dark place, but as I grew into adulthood and became a father myself, I recognized the action in love. The sacrifice of time for someone we care about. The compromise involved in ensuring someone else is comfortable in their environment. It had taken years, but I'd finally understood that everything was not about me.

And as I sat here in silence, watching Sasha's internal struggle with something she might never name, I made the decision to wait. It was obvious she wanted something from me. We didn't know each other, but she'd left an indelible impression on me. My reasons for pursuing a drink with her didn't really hold up anymore. *They never did.* Yet, for some reason, I felt drawn to her.

Feisty. Bold. Beautiful. Sexy. Sasha didn't let up. She saw right through my bullshit. But there was something else, something other than the obvious physical attraction, something deeper that made me want to give her what she needed. Perhaps it was because I could sense a sadness beneath the surface, a darkness inside of her. Maybe because that seemed familiar to me. The *whys* didn't matter, though, because none of this made any sense. And I suspected she felt the same way.

When she'd arrived several minutes ago, I'd offered her a drink. Which she'd declined. I tried to make small talk, which wasn't exactly my strong suit, but she barely responded. *Now, I'll wait.*

It didn't take long. She stood and paced my hotel room. Her intention to stall was clear. She spent several minutes staring at the ugly picture of horses on the wall, flipped the pages on the book I'd been reading, peered out the window, and finally turned to me.

"I'm not sure why I came here." She twisted in place and stretched a little. Then, she peeled off her gloves and rubbed her palms together. A moment later, she handed me a picture. "I don't trust easily." I met her gaze, but she rushed on before I could speak. "And I don't trust you. Not really. But I would like to hire you. I need help finding this man."

I studied the photograph. The image of a man leaning against a black truck smiled back at me. He didn't look like a criminal. He was dressed in khakis and a light blue sweater. His pants fit. He wore loafers. Appeared to be around eighteen years old. I flipped the picture over, hoping there was a date there. "Is this your daughter's father?"

She looked at me, her lips a hard line. "My daughter's father is dead. And I pray his soul is suffering where evil lives. In hell."

There was a story there, but I wouldn't pry. She'd tell me when she was ready. *Or not.* "Who is he?"

"My brother, Vincent," she explained. "The picture was taken ten years ago. I have other pics, more recent. I carry this one around because it brings me back to a time when he was happy."

"What happened?"

She blew out a deep breath. "A couple of years ago, my brother was shot and killed. It was a street assassination. Vincent and Shaun were only ten months apart, more like twins. Connected and close. When Shaun died, Vincent couldn't cope." She shrugged. "He was here one day, then gone the next. I haven't seen him since my brother's funeral, and I need to know if he's dead or alive."

In my line of work, I met many people who wanted to find loved ones. The reasons someone would leave their lives behind varied, but most of them were personal. They needed a change in scenery, wanted distance from toxic loved ones. Some made their decisions based on a physical threat. Some suffered from mental illness. Very rarely did I have to involve the police, but when I did, those cases were the worst. For Sasha's sake, I hoped her brother just needed to get away.

"What will you do if I find him?"

It was a question I asked all my potential clients. The last thing I needed was to lead someone to a long-lost relative, only to have them hurt or kill the person they were trying to find. A colleague of mine had lost his life facilitating an unwanted reunion between enemies.

Sasha dropped her head and picked at her thumb nail, before meeting my waiting gaze again. "I just want a hug," she admitted softly. "It doesn't even have to be a physical hug. It can be symbolic. I want to know if he's okay, if he's healthy, if he needs me."

The emotion shining back at me from her beautiful brown eyes was almost too much. Despite my behavior toward my family, I'd never had to deal with the loss of a sibling. I knew that if I decided to go home tomorrow, they'd be there waiting. I didn't pray much, but my daily prayers included one of protection for every person in my family.

I swallowed past a hard lump in my throat. "Understood."

"How much?"

Tearing my gaze from the photo, I peered at her. "Don't worry about it."

She shook her head. "No. I have to pay you."

"Okay. One dollar."

"I'll give you five-hundred dollars for services rendered. Because I don't accept free favors from men who might want something from me in return that I can't give."

"Fine," I conceded. "But I charge an hourly rate of seventy-five dollars per hour. Depending on the case, a typical missing persons locate runs around fifteen hundred."

Sasha's shoulder fell, but she held her head high. "Okay."

When she opened her purse, I placed my hand on hers, stilling her movements. "For you, I'll give you the family friend discount."

"What is that?"

I have no idea. Because if anyone in my family came to me and asked me to find someone, they'd expect me to do it for free. And, more than likely, I would. Shrugging, I said, "The discount is whatever you're willing to pay me. Or nothing."

She smirked. "Are you serious?"

"You met my family. Shit, Blake probably wouldn't even give me a dollar."

Sasha laughed then. "I can see your point."

"Listen," I stepped closer, but not too close, "one thing about me … I'll never make you do anything you don't want to do. I won't hold it against you or ever bring it up again."

Her expression softened. "Where did you come from?"

A smile tugged at my lips. "You don't even want to know."

She inched forward, coming so close to me I could feel the heat of her body. She was warm, like a heavy coat. "Maybe I do."

For the first time since I'd met her, I hesitated to do anything other than find her brother. I didn't lie to her when I told her I wasn't a player. It wasn't because I didn't know my way around a woman's body either. I preferred to keep my interactions with the opposite sex casual because I didn't have time to manage anyone's expectations. My focus had to remain on my daughter and my job. My daughter because she needed me. My job because I needed money to take care of Raven—and myself. Then, there was Demi. She was still a factor, for sure. But Sasha ... If I wasn't careful, this woman could consume me. Or burn me. Either one of those would wreak havoc in my life. I cleared my throat and moved away from her.

"Tristan," she whispered, her voice small but not unsure.

I felt her behind me and dropped my head. *She's making this hard.* "Yes?"

"You mentioned I could give you whatever I could pay. Five-hundred bucks. That's what I can pay."

Without turning to face her, I nodded. "That's fine. I'll invoice you."

"There's something else."

I peered up at the ceiling. "What is it?"

"Another reason why I came here tonight." She sucked in a deep breath. "I ... I need something else from you."

Closing my eyes, I finally turned. I raked my gaze over her face, committing to memory the flecks of gold in her eyes, the dainty point of her nose, her smooth skin, and those lips.

I raised a challenging brow. "Are you sure?"

"Very s—"

I captured her mouth with mine. The whimper that escaped her lips made me groan. The warmth of her body made me want to climb inside of her and stay a while. Spurred on by the intensity of the kiss, the way she responded to me, the way she let me take control, I backed her against the door. Gripping her chin in my palm, I sucked on her bottom lip until she moaned my name. Then I pulled back.

Her eyes popped open, the question in them. "What?"

Leaning in, I nipped her earlobe and whispered against her ear, "Is this what you want?"

Sasha shoved me away.

We stood there, eyes locked on each other, chests heaving. "Sasha?"

Then she tugged on the hem of my shirt and yanked me forward, back to her. Standing on the tips of her toes, she ran her tongue over my lips, placed a gentle kiss there, and bit down on my chin. "Does that answer your question?"

I whirled her around and nudged her to the door, so that her face was pressed against the hard wood. "Be careful what you ask for."

"You can stop talking now," she breathed. "I don't need your words. Just your dick."

I chuckled, stepping into her so she could feel my erection against that perfect ass. "That can be arranged, but first …" I reached around, unbuckled her pants, and pushed them down. Turning her back to me, I brushed my lips over hers again, dipping my tongue into her mouth. This time, I took it slow and easy, leisurely exploring her skin with my hands and my mouth as I unbuttoned her shirt.

Sasha's head fell back against the door. "Shit."

"Say please," I commanded, as I slipped my hand inside of her panties, cupping her pussy with my palm. But I held my hand still, didn't make a move. I needed to hear her beg for me, plead with me to let her come.

She gripped my hand, tried to force me to move, but I stood my ground. When I didn't give her what she wanted, her eyes popped open. "Please."

"Listen to me," I told her.

"What?"

"We're crossing a line tonight. I don't have to ask you if you understand that."

She licked her lips, and I followed the motion like a hawk. "I absolutely understand."

"But do you understand what this doesn't mean?" Using my thumb and forefinger, I pinched her clit gently.

"Oh yes," she purred.

"Is that an answer to my question, though?"

She glared at me. "Yes," she groaned, tightening her legs around my hand.

"Tell me."

"This doesn't change the nature of our relationship."

I slipped a finger inside of her, enjoying the satisfied purr that escaped her lips.

"When you make me come, I'll go home, and you'll find my brother."

I slid another finger inside of her.

She smirked. "We'll never mention this again."

I awarded her by strumming her clit with my thumb, winding her up until she called my name. "Good girl. What else?"

"No expectations," she breathed. "Now fuck me."

"Not yet. But I'll give you one." I continued my ministrations, letting her ride my fingers like I wanted her to ride my dick. "Are you close, Sasha?"

Her gasp was my only answer. I picked up the pace, applying pressure to her clit with my thumb as I fucked her with my fingers. She cried out her release before she came long and hard. When I was sure she was spent, once every tremble subsided and all was still, I stopped my movements yet again. "Beautiful," I said.

She opened her eyes. "Thank you for that."

"Anytime." I traced her lips with my finger, before taking it into my mouth and sucking it clean.

"Shit," she whispered. "That was hot."

Without warning, I gripped the thin fabric of her panties and tore them from her body. "I'll keep these."

Cocking her head to the side, her hair brushed her shoulders as she placed her hands on her hips. "What if I told you no?"

"Is that what you're telling me?"

She shook her head. "I bought them from Target anyway."

I barked out a laugh. "Good to know." Pulling her to me, I kissed her again. "I think I'll have you right here." I lifted her up, pinning her against the door again.

She pressed her mouth against my ear. "That works."

I grabbed my wallet and held it up to her, and Sasha immediately opened it and grabbed the condom that was tucked in a pocket. When our lips met again in an intense kiss, I pushed my pants down and slipped the condom on. Within seconds, I was inside of her. And ...

Damn. She felt good.

I stood there for a moment, enjoying the feel of her around me. But when her nails scraped along my back, I knew she was ready for me to move. Our pace was hard and fast as we raced to completion. Her grinding against me. Me fucking the shit out of her. And then she came once more, with me right behind her.

When I could move, I carried her to the bed and dropped her onto the mattress.

She stared at me with hooded eyes. "Again?" she asked.

"What do you think?"

Arching a brow, she beckoned me with her finger. "I think you're taking too long."

· · ·

Later, the only sound in the room was that of the furnace. After Sasha had come on my tongue several minutes ago, we'd retreated into our own thoughts. But neither of us made a move to get up, to burst the bubble we'd created. I could feel the walls forming between us, though. And I knew it was time.

Sasha sat up, pushing her hair back and peering over her shoulder at me. "I should go. Ola is probably worried."

I brushed my hand over her back. One last contact before she pulled away permanently. "Okay."

"Mind if I take a shower?"

"Do you."

She scooted to the edge of the bed, then disappeared into the bathroom. While she was showering, I pulled on my pants and jotted down some questions I needed her to answer so that I could get started on the search for her brother.

It didn't take long for her to emerge fully clothed. "The water pressure is pretty good."

I couldn't stand the small talk, but if she was comfortable with it, I'd go along. "Right." I handed her the piece of paper. "For you. If you could email me the answer to these questions about your brother, I'll get started tomorrow."

She stared at the paper. "Sure. I'll get on that." Once she'd tugged on her boots and coat, she sucked in a deep breath. "Thanks, Tristan."

"You're welcome."

"If I don't see you, Merry Christmas."

Then, she left.

In the past, I had no trouble compartmentalizing anything. But for the first time, I wondered if I could put Sasha in the never-touch-again category of my life. And *that* presented a problem. One that I wasn't sure had an acceptable solution.

Where It's At

Chapter Seven

LOVE ME OR LEAVE ME

Sasha

February, This Year

*S**o, I lied.*

I never pretended to be a bad liar. In fact, I'd mastered the art of bundling a little truth within a lie. I didn't feel bad about it either. I learned the hard way that words could breathe life or ensure death. Or in this case …

"Make. Me. Come."

I bit down on my lip to stop myself from screaming his name. Yet, as the inevitable pleasure he always provided rippled through me like waves, I couldn't help the low groan—*more like a whimper*—that escaped.

His soft, "Shh," brought me back to the present.

"Sorry," I gasped when he thrust into me again,

brushing his dick against that spot only he could hit. "I love your dick."

His dark eyes locked on mine and a smirk formed on his beautiful mouth. "Tell me again."

"I …" I gasped as he pounded into me. "Shit. I love …" I sunk my teeth into his shoulder as he continued to fuck me against the closet shelf, "your dick." I let out with a grunt. "I'm coming."

Again. Because he was a master at this. The way he commanded my body, the way he knew just what I needed every single time. It was almost too much to bear, but definitely too good to stop.

And the orgasm? *Damn.* It was delicious as it thundered through me, sending shivers outward to my fingers and toes. He pressed his mouth to mine, muffling my scream of appreciation. Seconds later, he came too, burying his face in my neck and sucking the sensitive skin there.

Silence enveloped us.

Then, like always, we retreated into the place that required distance between us. Each time we did this, it was harder to let him go. But I didn't dare say it, or even imply it. Because we set the rules a long time ago.

The lie?

It had been over a decade since I went to him at his hotel room, offered him a job, and then crossed a line with him. We negotiated the deal with every intention of following through. Yet Tristan … He was my drug of choice. I wanted to quit, I wanted sobriety. I also loved the way he made me feel. Drunk on him. Intoxicated by the fire we made together. Because I couldn't bring myself to follow the steps, to cleanse myself of this addiction.

I'd already admitted to myself that I was weak, that I was addicted to his dick. *To him.* I believed in a higher power. I knew that if I prayed hard and loud enough—and sincerely—God would help me. I had no problem giving up control. Except … instead of giving it to the Lord, I often gifted it to Tristan.

I have no shame. I absolutely blamed myself. And him. Taking a personal inventory. I did that every morning, before any of my clients came to me for help, and before I closed my eyes at night. I knew I was wrong. I considered it a flaw of my personality. I'd admitted it out loud. Granted, it was to my own therapist. But where I was stuck? Step seven. Asking Jesus to deliver me from this hold Tristan had over me. Because I wanted to lean into temptation. I wanted to drown in him.

Tristan rubbed my jaw with his nose, then brushed his lips against my skin. And just like that I wanted more. I wanted to do it again. *I want him.*

"I hate you," I whispered.

I felt the tremble of his laughter against me. And when he met my eyes, he raised a brow. "Do you really?"

No. "Maybe a little."

"You called." He winked. "I came. But not before you."

Rolling my eyes, I shoved him away. "I need a shower before our meeting."

He pulled my skirt up, twisted it around, and zipped it. Smacking my ass, he said, "Want me to join you?"

I fumbled with my shirt, struggling with the buttons. "No."

He swatted my hand away, taking over for me and easily buttoning the silk fabric. Then, he smoothed his massive hand over my breast, down my stomach, before he tucked the shirt into the waistband of my skirt. Resting his forehead against mine, he whispered, "You're all set."

I closed my eyes and sucked in a deep breath. "This is the last time." *I promise.*

"Okay."

Ugh. Every time he had to do something nice, something endearing when I wanted to keep our interaction businesslike, simple. Whether it was helping me up or making sure my clothes were right or fixing my hair when I looked a hot mess.

I brushed past him, opening the closet door and stepping into my office. Twisting around, I asked, "How did we end up in the closet again?"

I mean, we were in my locked office. My last client of the day had left over an hour ago. Ashlyn was on spring break with her friends. There was absolutely no reason to fuck in a dark closet. Well … other than it was hot.

"You were supposed show me something," he reminded me.

I snapped. "Right." I rushed back to the closet and grabbed the storage tube I'd brought in that morning. After handing it to him, I watched as he pulled the blueprint out. "The structural engineer finished this yesterday. I wanted you to see if before we met with your friend."

Okay, so I lied again.

I told Tristan I *only* wanted him to help me find my brother. Which he'd done in record time. As the years flew by, though, I'd come to depend on Tristan in other ways. What had started as a one-time, service-for-hire type of arrangement had morphed into a mutually beneficial semi-friendship. Simply put—I liked him as a person. He wasn't forthcoming. That old saying about pulling teeth to get him to talk … that was him. He rarely opened up about his feelings. But I was the same way. It worked for us. And we supported one another. When I needed him, he came.

He tapped his finger against the paper. "Is this where you want your house to go?"

I shifted closer to him, leaning in. "Yeah." I peered up

at him. "Do you think I should move here?" I pointed to another spot.

Tristan hunched a shoulder. "Maybe. I'd feel better if you and Ashlyn were on the far side of the property, away from the entrance. No one who doesn't live there should have direct access to you."

I nodded. "Good point." I picked up a pencil and circled the lot he'd suggested. "I just want to be a safe space for the women who will live here. I want *them* to have access to me."

He searched my eyes and brushed a stray hair from my face. "They will."

Averting my gaze, I pointed out another spot on the property. "I think security should be here."

"I agree." He stared at the map. "This is good."

I retrieved three more storage tubes from the closet. "I had copies made, one for you, one for Prescott Hayes Construction, and one for Caden." I grinned. "I'm so excited for this meeting."

He smiled. "You should be. You worked your ass off for this."

When I graduated with my masters degree, I immediately enrolled in a doctorate program to become a clinical psychologist. After my postdoctoral fellowship, I passed the licensure exam, and promptly relocated my family to Atlanta to set up my practice. Georgia had been the reset I didn't know I needed, a change in scenery and a fresh start in life.

Now that I'd been in business for myself for several years, I was ready to realize another dream of mine. Turned out my father was as much of financial genius as he was a selfish bastard, and he'd amassed a fortune. When he died last summer, he named me executor of his estate to my surprise. He had no debt, so my job was easy. Once I settled everything, I divided up the proceeds in equal portions for each of my remaining siblings and Leah, in Shaun's name. I used my inheritance to purchase a large plot of land outside of Atlanta and planned to repurpose another sizable piece of acreage near Detroit to develop tiny home communities for women who were misplaced for any reason or simply needed a safe space to live in peace.

The idea had come to me when Shaun died, and Leah was left with nothing because they weren't married. Then, when Ola left her husband after suffering through years of financial and physical abuse, she'd walked out with only the clothes on her back. I'd taken them both in with no questions, even though my situation wasn't much better.

After all, my relationship with Ashlyn's father was toxic. He was a tyrant and had terrorized me for years—until Carolyn handled it. To this day, I still had no idea what exactly she'd done. Once she stepped in, though, *he* backed off. That didn't mean he gave up. But I rested easier with the knowledge that as long as Carolyn was alive, I didn't have to worry about him. And when he died, a weight had been lifted off me.

"Did you tell the fam?"

Tristan had kept his word. He'd never made me feel like I had to do anything I didn't want to do. While I'd tried to keep Tristan from my little family, I wasn't able to do that because he'd offered strong support and invaluable resources to us through the years. *And sex for me.* With no questions asked or expectations of reciprocity for favors provided. As a result, Ola had grown to adore him, Leah considered him family. And Ashlyn? She loved him. He'd shown up for her, taught her how to ride a bike, and attended some of her volleyball games. He'd been a consistent male presence in her life, someone she could count on, and that alone made everything worth it.

"I talked to all of them on FaceTime last night. I wish they could be here."

Ashlyn was the only one who lived in Atlanta with me. Leah moved to Tampa and lived a boring life—as she called it—with her husband, my nephew, and their two kids. As a favor to me, Ola took a job working for Carolyn as her live-in nurse. Life hadn't been good to my former employer. After her divorce was finalized, she never fully regained her status in the community. Then, she'd lost her daughter, Trinity, to a car accident. Wracked with guilt, Carolyn had suffered a mental break. In recent years, she'd been battling several health conditions, including early onset Alzheimer's.

"I miss them." My heart clenched in my chest as I thought about them. It was quite an adjustment learning to live without Ola and Leah so close. We'd spent a lot of years together.

Tristan eyed me. "You can always hop on a plane."

I bumped my hip into him. "Shut up. Speaking of planes, when do you leave?"

He glanced at his watch. "After our meeting."

"Well, I guess I better get ready then." I shoved him toward the door. When I rented this office space, one of the lures was the on-site health center, equipped with top-of-the-line fitness equipment, showers, and lockers. I tried not to do it often, but sometimes I worked long hours and slept there. Having a shower in-house was a life saver. "I'll see you in an hour."

An hour later, we sat in a conference room downstairs. Another perk of the lease was access to shared amenities. The landlord was committed to providing smart work-spaces and had thought of everything when she designed the layout. Each office suite had a half bathroom, as well as an assigned storage area. As a tenant, we could modify our individual space to our needs using approved interior designers. In addition to the health center, the building had multiple phone rooms, a courtyard, a full kitchen, several conference rooms, a copy and print room, and a serenity room for times when we just needed a quiet place away from our desks.

I stared at my watch for the umpteenth time. "Do you think he got held up?" I asked Tristan.

"He'll be here."

Smiling, I turned to Tristan's brother-in-law, Preston Hayes, who was attending the meeting via Zoom. His partner, Cooper Prescott, was seated to my right. "Thanks for taking time out of your busy schedules to join me today. I'm looking forward to working with Prescott Hayes on this project."

Cooper smiled. "It was a no brainer. We're committed to making this work."

"That means so much to me."

The door opened behind me, and Caden Smith walked into the conference room. "Sorry I'm late. Atlanta traffic." He took the seat across from me.

I started with an overview of the project, outlining my goals for both properties. We segued into timelines, finalizing dates while considering potential obstacles such as supply chain issues. Caden took over, showing us designs of the models.

"Do you anticipate any delays in Atlanta, Caden?" Preston asked.

"No," he answered as he passed out leather-bound folders. "The county approved the plan this morning. We can break ground as soon as you get your construction crew down here."

As the men talked specifics, I watched Tristan. He stood in the corner like an imposing, unmovable mountain. Dark. Dangerous. And damn it … he was a challenge. Something to conquer. Something to climb. A place to hide. On the surface, he was a conundrum. A walking contradiction, a man most women avoided because there was no hope for anything lasting with him. But there were parts of him that were so sweet, so tender.

I wonder if anyone else has seen that side of him?

The ever-present scowl on his face ensured strangers gave him a wide berth, barely even making eye contact. He commanded every room he was in, made it known without saying a word that people should watch their step and their tone. And I loved it. Because his mere presence made me feel safe, secure. After a lifetime of feeling anything but, I needed that.

Real talk? I probably just needed him. I wasn't ready to admit that to him, though—or myself. Or anyone else for that matter. My family knew him, but the only person who knew I'd seen his dick was Tristan. And no one else had seen me naked since I started messing around with him. Which was fucked up, right? It wasn't like we were in a monogamous relationship. We were friends. We couldn't be more than that because everything about us was wrong. Except for the parts that were right.

Oh, God, this is a hot-ass mess.

Even if I wanted things to be different between us— *which I don't*—how would it work? Our families had no idea that we'd been entangled for all these years. Not even Paityn. Hell, for all I knew, Tristan could've had a whole family. A wife and a couple of kids. I wouldn't know because we didn't talk about *his* life. I knew his family because I knew Paityn. I knew he had a daughter because he'd told me, and I'd met her as the friend of her aunt. But

I didn't know where he slept when he wasn't with me. I didn't know who he spent his time with when he left my sight.

Do I want to know? I'd never ask, but yes. I suspected he was holding on to something, someone from his past. Raven's mother? *Or maybe Demi?* The question I'd asked him at Bar Louie had never really been answered.

A hand on my shoulder brought me back to from my thoughts. And when I swept the room and noticed he was no longer in the corner, I knew it was Tristan. He pressed his mouth against my ear. "Do you need a moment?"

I blinked. Then, glanced around the room only to find the men staring at me with interest.

What the hell just happened? I glanced up at him. "Maybe just one minute."

I raced to the door, opening it then shutting it behind me. Leaning against the wall, I buried my face in my hands and took some cleansing breaths. "Get your shit together, Sasha," I muttered to myself.

I heard the door click and waited. "Are you okay?"

Unable to look at him, I shook my head. "I'm fine."

He tipped my chin up. His expression softened. "You don't *look* fine."

"What did I miss in there?"

"Nothing," he explained. "Preston asked if you had any questions."

I counted to ten. Then to twenty. "I better get back in there, then."

He blocked me from leaving, caging me in with his massive arms.

Sighing heavily, I asked, "What are you doing?"

"Making sure you're good."

"Don't worry about me," I snapped. I peered up at the

ceiling and let out a heavy sigh. "I'm sorry. Just a lot on my mind." *And on my heart.*

He squeezed my shoulder, and I wanted to lean into him, breathe in his scent, drench myself in him. It wasn't the first time I'd felt that way around him, but it felt like it. I'd earned a living helping women realize what I'd been afraid to see myself. Now I was in the unfortunate position of not being able to control my emotions or even erect a wall to hide them. My ability to compartmentalize had faltered under the strength of my feelings for him. The truth was … After Tristan left to go back to his life, to do whatever he does, I would be here wishing I'd had the guts to ask him to stay.

Chapter Eight

FOOTSTEPS

Tristan

Growing up "Young," there was always an event, big or small. It could be as simple as Sunday dinner or a huge barbecue or a softball game. My parents always had something for us to do. Over the last few years, the number of weddings and baby showers seemed to multiply exponentially as my siblings started pairing up with the loves of their lives and procreating.

Paityn had started it off when she married young—no pun intended—then divorced a couple of years later. For both events, Ma threw a party. A wedding and a so-glad-you-left-that-clown brunch. Several years later, she met Bishop and now they were expecting their first child together. Bliss surprised everyone when she announced her pregnancy, but her baby's daddy wasn't shit. All of us wanted to beat his ass, but Blake was the one who actually landed the blows. Then, Blake met Lennox when she broke into his house to steal something she thought *he'd* stolen from someone else. Lennox proposed last year, and she still hadn't set a date. Next up, Dallas asked Preston to pretend to be her fake boyfriend for professional purposes. When they realized they weren't really faking it, they decided to make it official. She got pregnant, and they walked down to the courthouse to get married. Today, Dexter married his best friend, Char, giving Ma and her best friend, Maya, what they'd wanted since we were kids—a Young-Burke wedding.

At this rate, someone would announce a baby or an engagement in a few months. As far as kids … Shit, it could be anyone. And there were only four of us that weren't married. I was damn sure it wouldn't be me, so that left Bliss, Asa, and … Duke. After tonight, I'd bet money that he was next. His bride? Demi. Because I'd fucked up any chance I had with her with my bullshit.

"Daddy?" Raven approached me in the garden of the hotel where the reception was raging on inside. I'd been out here since I'd spotted Duke and Demi on the dance floor, declaring their love for one another for the world to see. "Are you going to stay out here all night?" She hugged my waist. "You okay?"

I smiled at my daughter. She was all grown up now. No more Daddy's little girl asking about farts and shit. When I looked at her, I was dumbfounded that she'd come from me. She'd exceeded all of my expectations, blowing me away with her intellect.

I wrapped my arm around her and kissed her temple. "I'm fine, Bubbles."

She leaned back, assessing me with knowing eyes. "Promise?"

I couldn't be prouder of the woman she was becoming —poised, competent, witty. She was a wiz in school and would be graduating with honors from University of Michigan in a few months. "I can't do that."

"Because you never lie to me."

It was one of the things I'd promised her a long time ago. No matter what, I would always tell her the truth. I remembered the day like it was yesterday. I knew I had a conflict on the day of her birthday party, but I told her I'd be there anyway. And when I didn't make it, she was devastated. Lika cussed my ass out because Raven had cried for hours that day and couldn't even enjoy her party. When she finally talked to me again, she made me promise to always tell the truth, even if I thought it would hurt her. Even at the young age of eight, she was more mature than I'd given her credit for. From that day forward, I always kept it real with her. Our relationship had thrived because of it.

"Is it because Demi is with Uncle Duke?"

"Not really?" I admitted.

"Even after the other day?"

Last year, I fucked up for the last time with Demi. We were in Atlanta at the same time for business, and I'd invited her out. I had every intention on showing up. Really. Then Sasha called. She needed me, and I made a choice that day. I chose to be there for Sasha. By the time I made it to Demi's hotel, Duke had already come to her rescue.

Still, I felt bad for hurting her again and decided to crash my siblings' annual *Young'Uns Weekend* retreat in Colorado. Needless to say, my presence was not needed or wanted. By any of them. And Demi had made it perfectly clear that I was out of chances. So I wasn't surprised when I showed up at my parents' house a couple of days ago and caught her leaving Duke's bedroom. It was obvious they weren't in there *talking* either.

"Demi deserves to be happy," I said with a shrug. I'd lost count of the number of times I'd had to say that since I'd been there. All of my siblings had managed to bring up the incident at one point or another. "Duke makes her happy."

"He really does," Raven agreed. "I love them together."

I couldn't say that yet. "I just hope he doesn't hurt her."

She shot me a sidelong glance. "If he does, what are you going to do? Fuck him up? Because from what Asa told me, you've hurt Demi more than anyone."

Damn. "Whoa. Are we really cussing in front of our parents now?"

She laughed. "Do you cuss in front of Gran and Pop Pop?"

"Point taken."

"I'm just sayin'," she continued. "The Cussing Jar is full to capacity at all times."

I handed her my fifth of cognac. "Since we're being adults out here, drink up."

"I was wondering if you were going to share." She took a sip and made a funny face. "You definitely don't have to worry about me being a Yak girl like Auntie B. Yuck! That stuff is nasty."

Chuckling, I took the bottle back. "Blake's been drinking Hennessy since she was a teenager, so don't feel bad."

"Anyway, instead of wallowing out here by yourself you should go inside and meet a nice lady."

I frowned. "What?"

She turned to me and picked up my hand. "I don't want you to die alone, Dad."

My eyes widened. "Wow. Do you think about that a lot? Me dying?"

Averting her gaze, she brushed her thumbnail over the wrought iron on the bench. "Sometimes," she confessed. "It's not like you work a regular nine-to-five."

Business was booming for me, and I'd had steady work since I started my firm. But I'd graduated from dangerous jobs a long time ago, focusing on contracts for several law firms and public agencies. "Don't worry about me, Bubbles. I keep my feet on the ground nowadays."

She tilted her head, staring at me with concerned eyes. "I want you to settle down. Find one place to call home so I can know where to visit you."

I brushed her cheek with my thumb. "There's always a phone call to ask me where I am."

"What happened to Atlanta?" she prodded. "Did you change your mind because of Demi?"

I brushed her cheek with my thumb. I owned real estate in several states because I traveled for work. Recently, I'd mentioned that I was looking to buy a home in Georgia. Apparently, Raven thought that meant I was moving there for Demi. Then again, my daughter didn't know about Sasha. "You're not going to let this go, are you?"

"No," she confirmed. "I told you … I don't want you to be alone."

"I'm not alone. Well, not really."

Her mouth fell open. "What? You have a girlfriend."

I scratched the back of my head. Up until this point, I hadn't told anyone about Sasha. The only reason my siblings knew was because Duke busted me out last Thanksgiving. He'd seen us together. But I could see the worry in my baby girl's eyes and wanted to ease her mind a little. "Not really. She's a friend."

"Seriously?" Her eyes lit up. "Can I meet her?"

Suddenly uncomfortable, I shifted in my seat. Because she'd already met Sasha. Granted, they didn't know each other well, but they'd been in the same space a time or two. "You already have."

She gasped. "Who is it?"

I cleared my throat. "I only told you that because I don't want you to worry. We're not together or anything. We spend time together occasionally. Sometimes." *And mostly to fuck.*

"But you want it to be more?"

Do I? The question hung in the air as I considered what it would be like to actually have more with Sasha. The nature of our relationship would change, but the idea didn't feel suffocating. If anything, the notion was appealing.

"Dad?" Raven called.

I blinked. "Huh?"

"Well? I asked you two questions. Answer both. Who is she? And do you want it to be more?"

I shrugged. "I don't know." Except, I knew I didn't want to let her go.

"What's her name?"

Scanning the area, I hesitated on saying her name because that would make this real. But I promised, so I said, "Sasha."

"Sasha?"

I turned to find Paityn standing behind us, one hand on her belly and the other holding a piece of cake. *Oh shit.*

"Hey, Auntie Tyn," Raven said. "Dad was just telling me about his friend. Wait a minute … Is this the Sasha that—"

Paityn raised a questioning brow. "Really?"

"Okay." Raven smacked her palms on her legs. "I hear

my song, so I'm just gonna go inside. Dad," she pointed at me, "I mean it."

I tossed her a mock salute. "Got it."

When Raven disappeared into the ballroom, Paityn took her vacated seat next to me. "Sasha, huh?"

"How long were you standing there?"

"Long enough." She cut into her cake. "Tell me everything, starting with why the hell were you ready to beat Duke's ass over Demi when you've been sleeping with Sasha for years?"

I took a sip of cognac. "That's not news to you. Duke blurted it out at *Young'Uns Weekend*."

She ate a piece of cake. "Yeah, but there was so much going on, I didn't get a chance to react. Now, I'm ready and waiting."

I struggled to figure how to tell the story without sharing too much, so I decided to give her the abridged version. "After you brought her to Thanksgiving dinner that year, we met for drinks and—"

"What?" she interrupted. "Are you talking about that dinner back in the day?"

I hunched a shoulder. "There was a connection. She hired me to find her brother, and—"

"You helped her find Vincent?"

"I did."

"Damn. You and Sasha can keep some secrets."

That's what I liked about her. I never had to worry about her telling anyone shit about me. "My work is confidential."

"Point taken," Tyn conceded. "Go ahead."

"Then we hooked up."

"And you've been hooking up for … what? Fifteen years? That's a long damn time."

It sounded ridiculous even to my own ears. I had a

relationship with Malika that only lasted a year and some change. Being someone's friend-with-benefits for longer than a decade seemed abnormal in a way. "Pretty much."

"Why aren't you two together?"

"Because the arrangement works. We see each other when we're ready. No expectations."

"That's some bullshit, brother. Everyone needs somebody. And you know I love sex, but there's more to life than getting busy." Paityn worked as a sex therapist and had started a line of naughty toys. "Take it from someone who used to have good sex with an asshole. It's not enough."

Except it wasn't really just sex between me and Sasha. She'd let me into her life. I knew her family. I spent time with them. *But I kept my life to myself.*

"Neither of us—" My words died on my lips because I didn't know what Sasha wanted from me long term. We'd never had the conversation. In the past, I could spot a woman who wanted strings a mile away, but she was good at hiding that part of herself from me. I figured it was because of her past relationships, which we hadn't delved into either. "Maybe things are good between us *because* we don't put all those expectations on each other."

"It's still bullshit." She shrugged. "And you know I hate that word. I've said it twice in less than five minutes."

I chuckled. "Whatever, Tyn."

"Tristan, do you like Sasha?"

"If I didn't, I wouldn't be with her."

"But you just said you're not *with* her," she pointed out.

"You know what I mean."

"No, *you* just need to mean what you say."

"What do you want from me?"

She set her plate down. "I want what Raven wants. I don't want you to be alone."

"She told you that?"

Tyn nodded. "All the time."

I dropped my head. "I do like her," I admitted softly.

"Of course you do." She stuck her tongue out at me. "Could you love her?"

I probably already do. "Let's just say I care about her, and I want to see her happy."

"You wanted to see Demi happy, too?" Paityn said.

"But I knew it couldn't be with me."

Tyn smoothed her hand over my back as I leaned forward, burying my head in my hands. "Honestly, I don't know what came over me at the house. Once I saw Duke with Demi, every competitive bone in my body screamed at me to pull her back. If Raven hadn't come upstairs, we would've been fighting. For no reason."

"Is that all that stopped you?"

"In the end, I couldn't do that to her." I wasn't sure which *her* I was referring to in that moment. Sasha or Demi. Or both. "Demi has always deserved more than I was capable of giving her."

"So why hold on?"

Am I an asshole for stringing Demi along for years? Absolutely. "I know I was wrong for how I treated Demi. I hate myself for holding on to her when I knew it would never work between us. Blowing into her life at crazy times, then ghosting her. It was fucked up."

In my warped mind, I thought I needed Demi's light to shine on me, so I didn't succumb to the darkness. I thought I needed the good in her to make me a better person. Eventually, I knew I'd fall off the pedestal she'd put me on, that she'd see me as the man I really was and that scared me. Because I needed to be her hero. I needed to be perfect for her, even though she never asked me to be that guy. I held on to her against both of our best interests. Especially when there was one woman who accepted me for who I was. No questions asked.

"You're scared."

I glanced at her. "Maybe."

"Demi represents redemption for you. She saw you as her heroic knight, and you latched on to that because you don't see yourself as worthy." She gripped the back of my head and forced me to look at her. "But you don't need to be redeemed, Tristan." She searched my eyes. "We love you. You just need to let us."

I closed my eyes and rested my forehead against Tyn's. "I love you, too." I hadn't said those words to any of my siblings in so long. The rush of emotion that shot through my body felt like it was going to destroy me with its intensity. I'd spent years running from them. Could I really go home and act like the last twenty-plus years never happened?

A tear fell from Tyn's eyes, and she dashed it away. "Boy, you know I'm pregnant. Stop making me cry."

I barked out a laugh. "Sorry."

She bumped my shoulder. "So what's next?"

"If I'm being really honest, I'd already accepted that it was never going to be me and Demi a long time ago. I accepted it because there *was* a me and *Sasha*."

I knew that from the moment I met Sasha in that bar all those years ago, from the moment she walked into my parents' house for Thanksgiving, from the moment I met her daughter, from the moment I sat across her at Bar Louie, from the moment I agreed to find her brother, and from the moment I made her come all over my fingers. Every single time, every single moment with Sasha only cemented that I couldn't let her go.

"Well," she stood and pulled me to my feet, "I think it's time for you to hop on that flight, brotha."

I hugged my sister. It felt good to unburden myself. "Thanks for this."

She peered up at me. "No, thank *you*. I'm just happy you finally opened up to somebody. I worry about you so much."

"Don't."

"You can't tell me what to do, man."

"I definitely can. I'm the oldest."

"In age. But we all know who the boss is."

I wrapped my arm around her neck and muzzled her hair.

She smacked me. "Boy, you know how much it cost to get my hair done?"

I cracked up. "The wedding is over. And since you love sex so much, I assumed you were going to let Bishop sweat that style out."

She gasped. "Don't play me."

We headed back into the ballroom, but she stopped before we walked inside.

I tilted my head. "What?" I touched her belly. "Is it the baby?"

"No. I was just wondering if this meant I could tell Sasha that I know about you two. You know I've been wanting to ask since Thanksgiving."

Shaking my head, I said, "Whatever, Tyn. Do you."

She grinned. "Thank you."

I skipped my goodbyes and caught the first flight I could find to Atlanta because …

I am who I am. I knocked on the door and waited.

A moment later, Sasha opened it. "Tristan? What are you … Shouldn't you be at Dex's wedding?"

"I'd rather be here with you."

She smiled. Then opened up the door and let me in.

Chapter Nine

HOW WE ROLL

Sasha

Three hours earlier

𝓘 stared up the ceiling, focusing on the piece I'd purchased this afternoon at an African Art exhibit in Midtown. The silk thread was vibrant, and I was drawn to the colorful yet bold image of three women at work.

"You can talk at any moment, Sasha."

I glanced over at Leah, who was seated in a chair next to me, her legs crossed and a pad of paper in her hand. She wore my wire-rimmed glasses and my new Allbirds flats. "Girl, you tried it." I sat up and smoothed a hand over my haphazard ponytail. "Take my shoes off."

"Sis, I thought we determined that you needed a therapy session. Let's go with it."

Shaking my head, I told her, "You're not my therapist."

My real therapist was out of town. Typically, she would make an exception for clients in distress, even while traveling. Much like *I* had done for my patients over the years. The rise of virtual therapy helped tremendously in that people had access to therapy wherever they were in the world. But even LaTonya had laughed in my face when I told her I needed an urgent session to talk about my dick supply.

Leah stretched. She'd come to Atlanta for the weekend because she supposedly heard something in my voice that indicated that I needed her. More than likely, she just needed a break from those kids. She had three of them, two under the age of eight.

"How about we just drink a bottle of wine?" I suggested.

Leah joined me at the breakfast bar. "I love your place, sis." She picked up a small sculpture I'd purchased last year at the Art Fair in Ann Arbor. "I just don't understand how you crammed all your shit in this box."

When I decided to build my own tiny home community, I knew I couldn't just talk about the benefits of living in a smaller home. I had to set the example to any woman who was hesitant about the choice she was making for her life. So I started researching builders in the area. Then, Tristan told me about his cousin.

My first meeting with Caden was productive. I learned that he owned a construction company and had to leave it behind for personal reasons. Now that he was in a better place, he was ready to get back to what he loved and wanted to focus on building affordable homes for people who needed housing but didn't have the resources to go the traditional route. He had the credentials, which included appropriate certifications and licensure to build. I loved that his mission aligned with my own and I appreciated his honesty about his troubles. After he showed me several models and incorporated some of my own ideas into a preliminary design, I signed a contract with him to build and deliver my house.

"I know. Remember when it was just a shell?" I asked, biting into a piece of chocolate. I plopped down on my sofa. "I couldn't even picture what it would look like finished, even with all the drafts Caden had sent over."

Leah joined me, kicking up her feet on the ottoman. "But all those tears were worth it in the end."

My Mighty House was four-hundred-twenty square feet of luxury living in a tiny shell. It was on wheels so that I could move it if I had to. I customized my home to fit me and Ashlyn comfortably and any guests that came to stay with us. There were two-stories, a master loft, a second loft for Ashlyn, a full kitchen, a living area, and plenty of storage. I wanted Ashlyn to have some privacy, so her room was on the other side of the house. It was also important to me that I had a dedicated work area so that I could work from home. To make sure it didn't feel cramped, I made sure I chose a model with high ceilings. I added a lot of windows and even had French doors installed.

Downsizing to a tiny home wasn't as difficult as I thought it would be. Because, for so long, we lived in a tiny apartment that wasn't much bigger than my current house. The biggest hurdle I faced was letting go of material things I didn't need anymore. I hired a professional organizer, and of course, my family stepped in to help.

I squeezed her hand. "Thank you for everything."

Leah sighed. "I would feel better if you'd just tell me what's wrong with you."

Resting my head on the back of the couch, I sucked in a deep breath. "I've been sleeping with Tristan." When I glanced at Leah, she was looking at me expectantly. "What?"

"Girl, I already knew that."

I gaped at her. "How?"

"You ain't slick, Sasha. All these years and you haven't mentioned being horny at all? I knew you were getting it in with someone. And you spend too much time with Tristan for it to be anyone else."

I smacked her with my throw pillow. "Really, heffa? I don't see Tristan that often."

"You see him enough. Besides, I can see. There's some hella chemistry between the two of you."

I shrugged a shoulder. "True."

"Anyway, what's the problem? Did you decide to stop seeing each other?"

We hadn't *decided* anything. After the business meeting with Caden, Preston, and Cooper, he left like he always did. And I hadn't heard from him since. "No," I replied. "It's just … I'm not sure how much longer I can do this."

"Because you met someone else?" she asked.

I shook my head. "It's not that. I haven't been anywhere to meet a man. I work. I come home and work some more. I spend time with Ashlyn, going to volleyball games and school events. We went prom shopping a couple of weeks ago. That was hard."

"She's going to junior prom?" Leah held a hand up to her heart. "I can't believe my baby is old enough to have a date."

I could still picture Ashlyn in diapers, toddling through the house, getting into all my plants. Next year, she would graduate from high school, and I'd be alone. Again. "She's going with her friends."

"Still … That's huge."

Tears formed in my eyes. "I know."

Leah rested her head on my shoulder. "You'll be okay without her."

I leaned my head against hers. "Promise?"

"Yep. That girl will check on her Mama if she doesn't do anything else." She sat up and took a sip of wine. "I hate that Junior doesn't get the chance to see you and Ashlyn often. He started his life with y'all. Sometimes, I regret moving him away."

"You have to live your life, Leah. Rodney is a good guy, an amazing father to all your kids."

"He aight," she grunted.

I smacked her hand. "He's more than that. And you have to know that Shaun would approve."

"Of Rod?"

"Of you being happy," I clarified.

"I still miss him."

"Me too." After Shaun died, I didn't think anything would ever fill the void his death created in our lives. It's still there, but time had healed my heart. "Something happened last week before Tristan went back to Michigan."

Leah frowned. "Did he hurt you?"

I patted her leg. "No," I assured her, "never that. But I looked at him and I wanted more than just sex. I wanted more than just friendship. But we're good the way we are. Can I mess that up? Should I say something to him?"

"Shit, you're the therapist," she scoffed. "You tell me. What would you tell one of your patients?"

I'd often struggled with following the advice I gave my clients. I became a therapist for several reasons, but one of the biggest was my own drive for redemption. I wanted to help others even though I hadn't really resolved my own issues. Just like an accountant could have financial problems, I had problems letting go of my past. I sometimes messed up when communicating with people I love. I was comfortable avoiding my problems. I told myself lies every day. Just this morning, I couldn't look at myself in the mirror without feeling resentful of my shortcomings. All those things made me who I was. If someone came to me and told me all of that, I would know exactly what to say to them. For some reason, I didn't believe my own words when it came to my life.

"I can't say," I admitted. "You know me. We've known each other since we were kids. We've seen each other through some crazy shit. I'm a little fucked up."

Leah cracked up, smacking her leg, and she fell over on the couch. "Sis, you're crazy for that. But yes! We all have a little of that in us."

"Or a lot," I countered.

She gave me a high five. "Well, I know you'll make the right decision. In the meantime, though, let's finish this bottle and watch a romantic comedy."

I stood. "How about we switch to tequila and watch a horror movie?"

"Whatever you say." She tucked her feet under the cushion. "Just know I'll be climbing into bed with you tonight."

We compromised on a thriller and settled in to watch it. But Leah fell asleep before the first act was finished. When the movie was done, she climbed into Ashlyn's loft for the night since baby girl was spending the night at a friend's house.

I washed the dishes and straightened up my living room. On my way to my loft, I poured myself a glass of water. A knock at the door drew my attention to it.

"Who the hell is that?" I muttered to myself as I

walked over to the door. Peering through the peephole, I paused. *Shit, he's here.*

I straightened my clothes, pulled the ponytail holder out of my hair, and fluffed my curls a few times. Then I opened the door. "Tristan?" I asked him what he was doing there. He was supposed to be at his brother's wedding, not standing on my porch.

"I'd rather be here with you."

My heart skipped a beat, jumped off my porch, and sprinted off a cliff at his admission. Which surprised the fuck out of me. Words escaped me, so I simply opened the door for him. *Oh boy. I'm in trouble.*

While I had designed my space so that Ashlyn could have privacy, I never expected to have a man in the house that I might want to fuck. Most of the time, Tristan and I hooked up at a hotel, in my office, in his car—or on any other hard or soft surface we could find that wouldn't result in our inappropriate behavior going viral.

Not to mention, Tristan had been very respectful about my space. Yes, he knew where I lived from the beginning. No, he never popped up unannounced. And definitely not after eleven o'clock.

"Have a seat next to me?" he asked, motioning for me to abandon my spot at the breakfast bar and join him on the couch.

I hesitated, glancing up at the loft where Leah was sleeping.

He looked up too. "Is Ashlyn here?"

I shook my head. "I mean, she's back. But she's not here. Leah is visiting."

"Oh." He nodded. "That's good."

He didn't seem bothered by Leah's presence, but he didn't exactly seem comfortable either.

I sat down next to him. "Are you okay?"

A moment passed. Then he leaned in. "Can we go somewhere?" He kept his voice low, presumably not to disturb Leah. "To talk?"

"Sure." I stood. "I'll just poke my head up there and let Leah know we're leaving."

"Bye!" Leah shouted from the loft.

I giggled. "I guess she heard me."

"You are standing right below me," she yelled.

Rolling my eyes, I motioned for Tristan to follow me to the door. After I locked up, I hopped in his truck with him. We drove for twenty minutes, toward Old Fourth Ward. Eventually, he turned into a gated community and headed toward the back of the property. He parked outside of a condo unit, got out of the car, and jogged around to open my car door for me. Without a word, I followed him to the front door. Seconds later, we were inside.

The place smelled new. The only piece of furniture in the living room was a leather couch. Curious, I asked, "Where are we?"

"My house," he answered, tossing his key on the kitchen counter. He walked to the refrigerator and pulled out two bottles of water. When he approached me, he handed me one of the bottles, then took a seat.

I scanned the room one last time before I sat next to him. "I didn't know you bought a house here."

"Last year."

Again, he'd left me speechless. I always assumed he traveled to Atlanta for business. I had no idea he actually lived here.

"There was something between me and Demi."

Jarred by the change in subject, I frowned. "What?"

"You asked me a question. Now, I'm answering."

I bit down on my bottom lip. In the beginning, I thought I had him figured out. He wasn't a typical man, by far, but he also didn't seem to be atypical. He never pretended to be a saint. And he always told the truth of the moment. Not necessarily *his* truth, though. We were alike in so many ways, but also very different. The fact that he answered a question I'd asked fifteen years ago …

I got nothing. So I didn't speak.

"Tonight, she told Duke that she loved him," he continued.

My eyes widened. I wanted to ask all the questions now, but I kept my thoughts to myself.

He rubbed the stubble on his jaw. "He loves her, too. She's happy. Which is all I really wanted."

"Tristan, I—"

"Up until recently, I led her to believe that *we* could be more than we were."

"How recently?" I asked, finding my voice.

"Thanksgiving weekend."

I thought back to last November. Ashlyn had broken her leg playing volleyball and I panicked when she had to go into surgery. I texted him on a whim, not expecting him to show up at the hospital to sit with me. We spent several days together, and he stayed through Thanksgiving before he left. "Are you telling me that Demi thought you two were together all the way up until three months ago?"

"We were never together, Sasha."

"Oh."

"But I didn't think I could let her go either."

"That's fucked up," I whispered as I fought against the anger that was settling in my bones.

"It is," he agreed.

"I'm trying to understand why you're telling me this

now. Because if this is supposed to be the prologue to me giving you some because you shared a piece of your soul with me, fuck you."

He met my eyes. "I deserve that."

I closed my eyes, angry at myself because he didn't owe me anything. We'd never made promises he didn't keep. But knowing that he was holding on to another woman while he was with me stung. I didn't know where we should go from here either. "I can't say I'm happy about the sudden need for you to tell me shit I don't really want to hear."

"You know me better than most."

My heart dropped. "I don't. Not really." I'd shared part of my life with him. I'd brought him around my family. But he'd kept so much of himself from me. Initially, it didn't bother me, but it did now.

"You don't know the specifics, but you see me. And you accepted me for who I am. You let me into your life."

"But you didn't let me into yours."

"You're right."

"So you said you didn't think you could let Demi go. Are you in love with her?"

"No."

I shot him an incredulous look. "Why did you lead her on?"

"Because I'm an asshole."

I sighed heavily. "That's honest."

"It's hard to explain, but Tyn said something today that resonated with me. I thought that Demi would ultimately facilitate my redemption."

"What do you need to be redeemed for, Tristan?"

"For making my family's life a living hell because I couldn't live with the truth of my parentage. And for almost killing Demi's father."

My mouth fell open, but I caught myself. "You …" I sat up straight, "what?"

"In a rage, I beat Alan Strong so bad, I could've killed him. And he wasn't the only one I took out my anger on. I've done things that I'm not proud of. I could've ended up in jail, but my father handled everything. Then, I enlisted."

"And you thought that Demi could redeem you?"

"I tricked myself into believing that if someone as good as Demi could love me, I must not be that bad of a person."

I scooted closer to him. "You're closed off. A little cocky. Opinionated. Intimidating. A smart ass. You're also funny. Kind. Giving. Dependable. Committed. Passionate. I would be able to name off more if you'd let me see all of you. Not just the soundbites. Not just what you think I want to see. You're not a bad person, Tristan. You've taken care of me and my family. You've shown up for me more times than not. If you were a devil, there is no way I would've let you around Ashlyn—or anyone else that I love. It's time for you to let that go. Forgive yourself. And work on your healing." He dropped his head, but I lifted his chin up.

"You don't know everything."

"You're right. I don't. I knew you were adopted." And not because he'd told me either. Over the years, Paityn had divulged many things about her family to me. While she didn't talk about Tristan a lot, she had confessed that she wished he'd come around more because she missed him.

"Paityn?"

"Who else would it be?"

He shrugged.

"After all these years, do you still think I talk to Duke?"

"Do you?"

One of the things I prided myself on was my ability to

stay out of people's business unless they paid me to be there. Duke and I shared a past through Carolyn because we worked for her around the same time. After Carolyn lost her business, I didn't have a reason to talk to Duke unless I was with Paityn. But that was a conversation for another day, and I refused to let him change the subject.

"I'm sorry," he whispered, pulling me closer when I tried to put a little distance between us. "I know you're not in contact with Duke."

"Good."

"He's a trigger."

"Because of Demi?"

"Somewhat."

"You mentioned you lashed out because you couldn't accept the truth," I continued, bringing the conversation back. I squeezed his knee. "How about we reframe it and admit that you were just a kid feeling normal emotions about a life-changing fact. I don't know what or how you found out, and you can't change the past. But you're an adult now, and you can control your actions. You don't have to treat your family like shit anymore. Relationships are hard. Even if you grow up in the same house with someone, you still have to work on being a contributing family member. Just like you have to work on being better every day. You can't bury your head in the sand and expect different results." I searched his eyes. "Still doesn't make you a bad person, though. I don't need to *know* everything to know that."

"Sasha …" He pulled me to him, hugging me tightly. "Thank you."

I brushed my lips over his temple. "You made mistakes. It's okay. We all do."

He leaned back, traced my bottom lip with his thumb.

I pushed his hand away gently. "Not so fast, Tristan. Are you ready to let Demi go?"

"Tonight, Raven told me that she worried about me dying alone."

Unable to help myself, I giggled. Ashlyn had told me something similar a couple of weeks ago. "They think we're old as hell, huh?"

"Yeah."

"She wanted me to go in the wedding reception and talk to a nice lady."

"Well … I guess that's a normal request." Especially since our liaisons were kept under lock and key.

"The thought of meeting someone else, being with another woman didn't feel right to me."

"What did you tell her?"

He shrugged a shoulder. "I told her I had a friend."

I sucked in a deep breath, steeling myself for the rest of the conversation. The air shifted as he pinned me with his intense stare. "Really? Who's that?"

Tristan smirked. "Sasha."

"Me? You told her about me?"

"I did."

My body flooded with warmth. "I don't know what …" I shrugged. "Never mind."

"I realized something a long time ago. But you already know I'm stubborn as hell and I couldn't admit it to myself even though I'd accepted it as a reality."

I couldn't look at him anymore, so I averted my gaze. Mostly because I was overwhelmed by the emotion swirling in his brown eyes. "What did you realize?" I picked at the hem of my shirt.

He gripped my thighs with both of his massive hands and tugged me closer. "I could've never been with Demi, even if she wasn't with Duke, even if I'd magically got my shit together long enough to commit to her. Once I met you, it's only been you."

My eyes fluttered closed at his admission. "Oh shit," I whispered.

He cupped my cheek, then brushed his lips over mine. "I'm not here because Demi's with Duke. You're not second choice."

Relief washed over me, and I slumped forward, leaning my head against his chin.

He kissed my brow. "You're *the* choice. *My* choice. And I've made it every single time."

I lifted my eyes. That bomb felt like it decimated all our pretenses that this was never going to be more than what it was. I had so many questions. When did he choose me? Did Demi know about us? "Tristan, I—"

"I know we have a lot to talk about, a lot to learn about each other, but not now. I don't want to talk about Demi or anything else. I just want to lose myself in you. I want tonight to be about us. Is that okay with you?"

Once again, I couldn't find my words. But damn … Forthcoming Tristan could get it. And he would. All night. Nodding, I kissed him, effectively surrendering to him, offering him the reprieve he needed for the night. He stood, picked me up, and carried me upstairs. At the sound of his shoes on that hard wood, something occurred to me.

"Wait," I shouted.

He stopped. "What is it?"

"I hope there's a bed up there because my neck and my back cannot get down on this floor."

Tristan barked out a laugh. "The bed is upstairs."

I kissed him, sucking his bottom lip into my mouth until he groaned. "Good to know."

Chapter Ten

WALK ON BY

Tristan

*R*ight around my tenth birthday, Dad took me out for what he called "Young man to man" time. Before we left, Ma prepared a feast of a lunch, which included my favorite foods. When we set out, I had no idea where we were going, but I remembered being excited about the possibilities.

The day turned out to be better than I could've anticipated. We started with breakfast at Big Boy Restaurant, which was my favorite. Then, we embarked on our journey. Our destination was Lake Erie. Our activity was fishing. While we waited for that first catch, we talked about everything that was important to me—NBA Jam, Mortal Kombat, and that Apple computer I wanted for Christmas. I was a gamer and there was not much that was more important than my Super Nintendo or my computer. Once I'd talked his head off about that, the conversation shifted to Angel Ward, the little girl who kept yelling at me during recess. I vented about how she told the entire class that I was her boyfriend and then demanded that I spend my allowance on her. Even at that age, I was extremely budget conscious. Giving a girl money for no reason wasn't going to work for me, especially since I had my eye on the new Streetfighter game.

Dad had listened to me intently, then he told me, "*One day, you're going to want to be someone's boyfriend. And you'll give her all your money just to see her smile.*"

I didn't believe him. But now …

As my gaze raked over Sasha's naked body, from her toes to her thick thighs to her stomach to her full breasts to her mouth, I knew he was right. I wanted to be hers. I wanted to give her everything. All of me. All my money.

"Tristan?" Sasha straddled my lap. "What's on your mind?"

I kissed her, dipping my tongue into her mouth and sucking on her tongue until she groaned. "You," I admitted, nipping at her chin.

She searched my eyes and ran her finger down the side of my face. "I don't believe you."

I raised a brow. "You're sitting on my dick. What else would I be thinking about?"

Wrapping her arms around my neck, she rocked into me. "Don't change the subject."

I flipped her onto her bag, resting my body on hers. "Just thinking about something my father told me."

She lifted a questioning brow. "Now?"

I brushed my mouth over hers. "He told me that one day I would want to give a woman my money."

Giggling, she said, "Did he?"

"Long story."

"Do you want to give me your money?"

I barked out a laugh. "I mean … I *would* if you—"

She kissed me. Hard.

"What was that for?"

"Because. By all accounts, you're stingy. So I'm counting that as a win."

I wrapped her legs around my waist, pressing my dick against her core.

"Wait." She bit down on her bottom lip. "This isn't right."

Confused, I pulled back. "What?" I could sense the air shifting around us.

"I can't have sex with you tonight."

My stomach roiled as I thought about all the potential reasons she didn't want to be with me tonight. Change of mind? *Change of heart?* It could've been anything. We'd known each other for a long time, but maybe my truth was too much for her. "What's wrong?"

"Nothing."

I rolled onto my back. "Now I don't believe you?"

Sasha made no move to get dressed. Instead, she sat up and leaned her back against the headboard. Glancing over at me, she sighed. "I'm serious. Nothing is wrong. It's just … You flew to Atlanta after you had this big epiphany about me."

I perched myself up on an elbow. "Right."

"You said you wanted to just be with me." She tucked a strand of hair behind her ear. "And just for the record, I want that, too."

Downstairs, I'd basically dumped all my shit on her. After I left the wedding, my singular focus was to get to her. I didn't stop to ask her what she needed from me. I didn't even think of what would happen if she wanted something different. "Good to know."

She smirked. "It's crazy, but I also had an epiphany."

The urge to pull her closer, to touch her, to kiss her hit me. But I also wanted to respect that she obviously had something to say. I wanted to show her that I was willing to do whatever she needed. "Tell me more."

"The last time I saw you, during the meeting with Caden and Prescott Hayes …"

When I left town, I assumed the project was full steam ahead. I'd already heard from Den that he got the final approval from the County. And Preston had pulled me aside during the wedding festivities to let me know that he would personally be at the site when they broke ground.

"Yes?" Unable to help myself, I brushed my hand over her bare thigh. Bending down, I nipped her soft skin, then soothed it with my tongue. Her sharp intake of breath let me know she wanted my touch, which eased my mind. "Are you having second thoughts about anything?"

She swept her thumb over my bottom lip. "No. I'm so excited about everything."

Sasha had shared her dream of building a haven for women, and I'd supported her from the beginning. We'd brainstormed ideas on execution. My brother-in-law, Bishop, had even assisted her in developing a business plan. After her father died, she'd come to me and told me she was ready. I knew that Caden had been slowly trying to rebuild his life and had an interest in alternative housing, so I contacted him and Preston. The rest was history.

Thinking about how this all came to fruition high-lighted the role we played in each other's lives throughout the years. Sasha was right. She'd brought me into her world, introduced me to the people closest to her, trusted me with her dreams. Although I suspected there was still a lot I didn't know about her, I knew a hell of a lot more about her than she did about me. And if I wanted that to change, I needed to be open about my life as well.

"While they were talking," she continued, "I thought about you."

"What about?"

"About how you were there. You've been there for me. Watching over me, making sure I was good. It's been that way since I met you. Which is strange because we've never talked about it, or even acknowledged it. But that doesn't make it any less true. You've been the man in my life. I guess when I think about it, I haven't wanted to date or see anyone else because I had you."

"How do you feel about that?"

"It's hard to describe. But for the first time, I felt like it wasn't enough for me." She laid on her side, turning to face me. "I don't want you to stand on the perimeter of my life anymore. And I don't want to stay on the periphery of yours. I want to share everything with you. If this is going to work, we both have to agree to work at it."

I cupped her cheek in my palm and kissed her once. Then another time. "I want that, too."

"I'm glad to hear that."

"What do you need from me?"

She grabbed my hand and entwined our fingers. "I think we need to reset this relationship. We need a pause."

"Wait, I—"

"One thing we know how to do well is sex. We're definitely compatible in that aspect."

I chuckled. "That's a fact."

"Let's take that out of the equation."

I raised a brow. "For how long?"

"Tristan!" She shoved me playfully. "Don't look at me like that."

I wasn't sure how I was looking at her, but I knew how I felt at that moment. *Horny*. But as much as I wanted to immerse myself inside of her warmth, I also had to admit she had a point. "I'm sorry. You're probably right."

"How about we spend some time in the light, go on a date or two. Talk about any and everything. I want Ashlyn to know that you're more than a friend. And I want Raven to know me as your girlfriend, not just Paityn's friend."

"That's fair." I sighed. "But you know this is hard for me. I don't share easily. Can I ask for your patience while I'm still figuring shit out?"

She smiled. "Of course."

"Thank you." I pulled her to me, taking in her scent and enjoying the feel of her body against mine. Because only the Lord knew when I'd get another chance. When my dick stirred, I knew that was my cue. I grabbed the comforter at the end of the bed and draped it over her, tucking her in tightly.

She cracked up. "Really? You know I can't sleep like this. Night sweats are a thing at my age."

"I'll get you a shirt."

"You actually keep clothes here?"

"Ha, ha. You got jokes, huh?"

"I'm just sayin'." She poked her arm out of the comforter, giving me a glimpse of her breast. And one nipple that begged for my attention. "I don't see a dresser or anything. A chest?" She peered over my shoulder. "That closet looks as bare as the bottom level."

I tugged the blanket over her again. "Don't worry." I got up and walked into the closet. A moment later, I returned with a T-shirt and tossed it at her. "Put that on."

"Fine." She sat up, letting the cover fall to her waist. "Even though I sleep naked, I'll put this on for you." She gestured to me. "You need to put something on, too, playa. Looking all ready for me."

I couldn't help but laugh. "Point taken." I tugged on a pair of sweats and joined her on the bed.

She burrowed into my side. "This feels good."

Damn good. This wasn't the first time we'd spent the night together, but it was the first time we'd spent the night together as more than fuck buddies. "Reminds me of that night we were stuck in Boyne."

I felt the tremble of her laughter against me. "Except for snow."

A couple of years ago, Sasha's car had broken down right before she was scheduled to go to Boyne Mountain for a seminar. When she called me, I came. There was no time to take the car to the repair shop, so I offered to drive her up north. Unfortunately, we drove into a mini blizzard. The blowing snow reduced visibility and I had to pull over. We ended up finding an old motel and making the best of it. All night.

She giggled. "Remember we had to clean your car off with our hands because you broke the brush?"

"Don't remind me," I groaned. "I can still feel that cold years later."

"We've really been through some things together," she mused.

"Right?" Earlier, she told me I was the man in her life. She was the woman in mine. Able to get me to do some shit I swore I'd never do with one look in her eyes. "I just couldn't stay away from you."

"Now you don't have to." She shifted so she could face me. "You can rest in me, Tristan."

I gripped her chin, pulling her to me. "Are you sure you're ready for me?"

"I love a challenge. And I'm not scared."

"Sure?"

"You always ask me that."

"Because I need you to be sure."

"You're not the only one that has a past," she said. "There are things that you don't know about me."

Sasha had alluded to something dark in her past, something that had changed her perspective on life. I was always careful not to pry. I also never tried to dissuade her from telling me anything. "I understand," I assured her. "Just so you know … Nothing you ever tell me will change what happened here today."

"Sure?" she asked, throwing my own word back at me.

"Positive."

When our lips met, I kissed her with everything I had, trying my best to pour every unspoken emotion into it. I wanted to give her every assurance that this was real. I only stopped to breathe before I went in for more. Her soft moans gave me her approval, and I had to fight hard to stop, but finally I did.

"Sasha," I murmured.

She placed wet kisses along my jaw. "Hm."

I bit her chin gently. "I'm trying to be respectful, but …"

"Mhmm." She sucked my earlobe into her mouth and nipped the lobe. "What is it?"

I rolled her onto her back, pressing my erection into her. It would've been so easy to sink into her, to consummate this change in relationship status. "Damn, baby. This is hard."

"It is." She gripped my dick in her palm and squeezed. "Maybe I spoke too soon," she said breathlessly. "We can reset tomorrow."

As appealing as that was, I wasn't going to let our emotions get the best of us. "No." I buried my face in her neck and whispered, "When we do come together again, I don't want you to have any doubts. The time has to be right."

"Okay," she moaned, pulling away. She covered my chest with the same comforter I'd used on her earlier. "Put your muscles away."

I barked out a laugh. "You're silly for that."

"It is what it is." She leaned into me again.

We settled into silence. "Good night, Sasha."

"Night, Tristan."

As she drifted off to sleep, I finally felt free enough to do exactly what she'd told me to do. Rest.

Sasha

"Are you sure you want to do this?" I glanced over at Tristan. We'd spent the morning in bed talking. It felt good to just lay with him. No rushing. No shitty excuses to leave. Just us.

Waking up next to him, eating together … it felt like a new experience. It was surreal. The conversation didn't veer to anything serious, we simply chatted about our week like we'd done many times. Instead of politics or sports or even food, though, we talked about personal stuff. He told me about his trip home, about his upcoming job. He revealed that he'd enjoyed being around his family, but he was often uncomfortable when all of them were together. It made sense. The Young family was a lot. I wasn't around them much, but even I had felt overwhelmed at a function or two. But I was glad when he told me he wanted to try to rebuild his relationships with his siblings.

After we had a small breakfast of dry cereal—that was the only edible thing he had in his house—he brought me home. When we arrived at my house, I half expected him to leave like he'd done in the past. I was pleasantly surprised when he put the car in park and escorted me to the door.

Ashlyn's Toyota was there, which meant she'd cut her sleepover short. I imagined she and Leah were inside watching some reality show. Introducing Tristan into the mix could prove to be interesting.

"You don't have to come in," I said.

"I'm good, Sasha." He squeezed my shoulders. "But we can take this as fast or as slow as you need."

I wrapped my arms around his waist and rested my forehead against his chest. "I don't know what's wrong with me," I mumbled into his shirt. Glancing up at him, I said, "This just feels big."

"Because it is."

"What if …" I nibbled on my bottom lip. "It was perfect when we were alone. Now we're bringing people into the bubble."

"Are you worried that Ashlyn won't be happy?"

I'd be lying if that hadn't crossed my mind, so I told him as much. "She's never seen me with anyone."

Other than Tristan, I'd avoided bringing men into our space. Growing up like I did, I'd seen firsthand the trauma strangers—or even close family members—could inflict on little kids and I was careful not to expose Ashlyn to anyone I didn't deem safe.

"Never?" he asked.

"When did you think I had time to go out?"

He shrugged. "I don't know. I assumed that you dated casually."

"Did you?" I held my breath, awaiting his answer.

Because I didn't know what the hell I would do if he told me he'd been dating while I was … not.

"Nah. I didn't have to."

I released a sigh of relief. "Exactly. Because you were already getting some from me."

"Pretty much."

"So … this is going to be an adjustment for her. For us."

The door swung open behind us, startling me. "Mom!" Ashlyn stood there, hand on her hip. Leah was behind her. "You can come in now." She smiled at him. "Hi, Tristan."

"Hey, Ash."

I stepped into the house. It wasn't exactly the walk of shame, but it was something similar. "Hi." I gave Ashlyn a kiss.

Tristan brushed past me and took a seat on the couch next to Leah like he didn't have a care in the world.

"When did you get back?" I asked my daughter.

"About an hour ago," Ashlyn said. "I came back early to spend some time with Leah. I thought we could go to breakfast or something."

"Did you already eat?" Leah asked Tristan.

"Cereal," he replied. "But Sasha is probably still hungry."

I set my purse down on the countertop. "It was more of a snack because he didn't have any milk at his place."

Ashlyn glanced at Tristan. "You live here?"

He shrugged. "I have a house here."

My daughter smiled. "That's good to know." She sat in the small recliner situated next to the breakfast bar. "Does that mean we'll be seeing more of you?"

I gaped at my daughter. "Ashlyn," I chided.

She shrugged. "What? Mom, you spent the night with

him. I caught you in an embrace on the porch. It's obvious there's something going on."

Leah sipped her coffee. "Been obvious for a long time," she muttered.

Tristan shot her a sidelong glance, then turned to Ashlyn. "Would you be okay with that? With me coming around more?"

Ashlyn placed her hand on his shoulder and nodded. "Tristan, I think it's safe to say that I trust you as a man. You've been clutch. For real. In fact, I hit a pothole this morning on my way home. Can you look at my tire?"

"I got you."

Giving him a thumbs up, Ashlyn handed him her car keys. "Anyway. As much as I love the idea of my mom getting her groove back, the jury is still out on if I trust you as my momma's man."

Watching my daughter lowkey interrogate Tristan was a treat. I always loved their relationship. There was mutual respect, for sure. But there was also a sweetness in their interactions. I figured it was because he was a father himself. He knew how to talk to her. And she was right … He'd saved the day on more than one occasion.

"That's fair," he said.

"Even so," she continued, "if my mom has to date someone—finally—I'm glad it's you."

When he met my gaze, his expression softened. "Me too."

"I guess I'll just slide in here with an opinion." Leah set her mug down. "Real talk. You already know."

He nodded. "I do."

Confused, I asked, "What do you know?"

"Don't worry about it, sis," Leah said. "As long as Tristan knows, we're good."

"Tell me," I insisted. "Have you two been talking about something?"

"It doesn't need to be said," Tristan explained.

Leah gave him a dap. "Because … I'll die for mine."

The lightbulb went off and I finally recognized what hadn't been said. Leah was my sister in every way. The unspoken message was clear. If Tristan hurt me, she'd go out in a blaze of glory to protect me. Full stop. It was exactly the type of conversation I'd had with her husband before they got married. I didn't play about my family.

I sat on Leah's lap, hugging her. "Aw, sis. I love you, too."

"Girl!" Leah shoved me aside. "Sit on your man's lap, damn."

"Which leads me to my next question," Ashlyn said. "This house is not big enough for Tristan."

He barked out a laugh.

I gasped. "Ashlyn!"

"Mom, this is a tiny house." She gestured to him. "He's not tiny."

Leah snorted. "Shit, I'm small and sleeping in that loft was kind of tight."

"It's not that bad." I elbowed Leah. "You said it was comfortable."

"For a weekend," she clarified. "Not forever."

"Look at his legs," Ashlyn screeched. "Real talk, he could probably move this house with his bare hands."

Tristan wrapped his arm around me. "It's fine."

"I have the perfect solution," my daughter announced. "When you move into Tristan's place, you can pass this place down to me when I graduate."

I cracked up. "I know you lyin'. I love my house."

And I'd worked hard for it. With all the changes going

on, I hadn't thought about how this new relationship would affect my living situation. The house was the perfect size for me and Ashlyn, but it wasn't set up for a third person.

"Besides," I added, "we're not at the moving-in stage yet." I elbowed Tristan, hoping he'd jump into the conversation. But he sat in silence. "Right, Tristan?" I prodded.

"I don't think we're moving in tomorrow," he agreed. "But I don't think it's wrong to consider the logistics of a potential move-in situation either."

My eyes widened. *This man* …

If I had any doubt that he was serious about me, this talk had removed it. "Really?"

He shrugged. "How long does it take to make a decision? We'll know when we know. Until then, we make it work."

"My dog," Leah said, giving him dap. "I knew I liked you for a reason."

"You could always buy a not-so-tiny home and park it right next door," Ashlyn suggested.

Leah snapped. "Good idea, baby girl."

Oh God. Still, I couldn't help but smile because this was what I wanted. When I thought about being with Tristan, I wanted the family time, the in-house laughter, the jokes. I wanted it to feel normal, I wanted it to feel safe. Today was all those things, and I was extremely grateful. For the first time in a very long time, I believed that I could have it all —my daughter, a career that I love, and my man.

Chapter Eleven

GOOD & PLENTY

Sasha

"*I*'m going to fall."

The first time my foot slipped, I screamed like a banshee. The next time, I cried for Jesus to come save me from my bad decisions. And the third time, I was just done.

"You'll be fine," Tristan assured me. "Just let go."

I wrapped my fists around the harness and tugged. It was on tight, but I couldn't be sure. What the hell was I thinking climbing a damn rock like I wasn't afraid of heights? "I can't do it," I shouted, holding on to the tiny knobs on the rock. I looked behind me and yelped. "Oh my God."

"Sasha." Usually, his voice offered me comfort, ushered in a feeling of safety. But today it did nothing for my anxiety.

I squeezed my eyes shut. "This is your fault."

He laughed. "How?"

"Because you told me I couldn't do this, and you know I'm competitive." That was something we had in common. We both hated to lose. Especially when there was money on the line. Yep, I bet him fifty bucks that I could climb his favorite wall. At this point, I would've given him a hundred if he rescued me.

I called for help, knowing that no one would come to save me. When we were trying to decide what to do for the day, I mistakenly told him to choose something he liked to do. So he called in a favor and arranged a private rock-climbing activity. Arriving at Rock With You Indoor Climbing Gym, I took one look at the wall in question and immediately agreed to do it. Oh, I talked mad shit, too. Told him I would walk away with money toward my pedi-cure. Even knowing that I had a hard time crossing a bridge in a car. I hated to look out of the windows if I was on a top floor. I rarely stood out on a balcony. And forget glass floors or elevators. I couldn't even take the simulated Soarin' Around the World ride at Disney Land. So, again ...

Why am I here?

Luckily, Tristan was a certified Belayer and had once worked as a climbing instructor for fun because he loved it so much. But even though I knew he wouldn't let me die, I was scared as fuck up on this wall.

"Baby, look at me." His voice pulled me out of my thoughts. "I need you to watch me."

I shook my head. "No."

"You have to open your eyes. If you fall wrong, you could hurt yourself."

"I'm too damn old for this," I mumbled.

"Sasha," he called again, "look at me."

My heart was pounding in my ear as I contemplated

my next step. *And now I have to pee.* "I have to get down," I whined.

"Look at me." I felt him next to me and I jerked away, letting go of one of the rocks.

Yelping, I struggled to grip another one. "Where did you come from?" A few minutes ago, he was on the ground, encouraging me to keep going.

He grabbed my hand.

"I can't do this."

"Yes, you can. Watch me." He placed my hand on the holder. "Just walk down like you walked up. And when it's safe to fall, I'll let you know."

Nodding rapidly, I whimpered, "Okay."

It took ten more minutes of him pumping me up for me to take one step down. My arms were on fire, but Tristan coached me through the descent, encouraging me along the way. When I made it closer to the bottom, he dropped down. "Okay," he said. "Come on."

I sent up another silent prayer and stepped down. My foot slipped, and I cried, "If I fall, I'm going to kill you."

"You're not going to fall."

I kept going. And when I finally got low enough for him to touch me, he grabbed me. Feet now firmly on the ground, I took a few calming breaths before I rushed to the restroom. When I returned, I leaned against the wall. "Never. Again."

He chuckled. "You did alright."

I glared at him. "Don't lie. I suck at this."

"I wouldn't lie to you. The climbing technique was there. If you would've told me that you were afraid of heights, we could've gone bowling or something."

"I thought I could conquer my fear."

He frowned. "Why not try that on the SkyView?"

The SkyView Ferris Wheel was a popular attraction in

Atlanta. I'd been there for years and had yet to purchase a ticket. And I had no plans to do so. "Are you crazy?" I bellowed. "I'm not getting on that thing."

The smile that formed on his lips and the wicked gleam in his eyes made me uncomfortable. "Sasha …"

I held up a hand to stop him from coming closer. "No."

"Just once."

"No," I repeated. "I'm not going."

He inched toward me.

"Stop."

He reached out for me, but I dodged him, ducking under his arms and bolting to the other side of the room. He chased me, catching me easily and swinging me in his arms. I screamed, but this time it was with delight and not fear. Without a word, he hoisted me over his shoulder in a fireman's carry. "Let's get you changed."

"I'm more than happy to change, but not for that Ferris wheel."

"Alright, alright," he said. "We can grab lunch."

I smacked his ass as he walked me to the locker room. "My choice, since I survived."

An hour later, we were seated—on ground level—at a table at Biggerstaff Brewing Company. Tristan's choice. He was a beer-and-burger type of guy, which I loved because I was in heaven around all the fried food.

I leaned forward, linking my hand with his. "I hope you know I'm not going to be able to move tomorrow."

A sly grin spread across his lips. "I told you to start small. You could've climbed the other wall."

And I would've. If he hadn't told me that it was the same wall that they started little kids on. Then, he'd admitted that Raven had started when she was five years old. Five!

"Shut up," I grumbled, taking a sip of my beer.

"It's okay." He swept his thumb over my palm. "You can't win at everything."

I snorted. "I can win at most things."

He chuckled, and I couldn't help but smile. Hearing Tristan laugh was a treat because I know he didn't do it often. I'd heard it more in the last two weeks than I ever had and that made me feel good. The last couple of weeks since we'd made the decision to move forward together had been basically business as usual. Except for the kisses and the open affection in public, whether it was just in front of Ashlyn or at a restaurant or a bar.

The segue into this space felt natural. But what didn't feel natural was the fact that I hadn't sat on his dick in weeks. We'd always had a healthy sex life—without the expectations. Now that we'd redefined our relationship, now that we were an official "thing," the pressure was on. Thinking back to the night he'd come to me after his epiphany, I couldn't help but worry that the awkwardness I'd felt in the bedroom would return once we decided to make love.

"What do you have a taste for?" he asked.

I perused the menu. "Have you eaten here before?" Everything looked good, but the crispy Brussel Sprouts and shrimp rolls were calling to me. "I feel full just looking at the menu."

"It's close to my place, so I've been here a few times for breakfast. The smoked brisket breakfast sandwich is good."

I groaned. "We have to come back for breakfast one day."

"On a cheat day?"

My chest tightened, and I felt a blush sweep across my

face. "You got jokes, huh?" I dropped my head on the table, before meeting his amused gaze again. "I can't believe I ate all of that." Yesterday, I'd confessed that I needed help getting back on my healthy eating kick. Then, I proceeded to eat a whole plate of truffle fries and fried chicken wings. When he questioned me about my choice, I told him to leave me alone because it was a cheat day.

"I think it's funny. I love that you eat real food."

"Not every day," I lamented. "I would like to be able to fit my clothes."

His gaze dropped to my mouth and then lower. "If you can't … That's fine with me too." He traced my fingers with his thumb.

The contact against my skin combined with the heat blazing from his eyes consumed me from the inside out. In just a few seconds, he'd put me in a spell, and I was no longer hungry for food. My body was screaming at me to cut lunch short, to let him take me … home. Or to his car. Or the bathroom.

The waitress delivered our beers, effectively dousing the steady fire building in my gut. I blew out a deep breath and forced a smile on my face. Once we placed our orders, I looked at Tristan again and changed the subject to construction. Caden had called last night to let me know that we needed to push the start date back due to a problem with a supplier, but he assured me we would still finish on time.

"I've been thinking about staging," I announced. "I want to have a model that prospective owners can rent before they make the final decision to buy. So I've been thinking of ways to decorate. Not just inside, but outside."

"Makes sense. Curb appeal is an important selling point."

"Exactly. I'm considering a partnership with Rob."

The company who'd designed my rooftop deck was ready and willing to help. I'd known Rob for years. We actually grew up together in Flint, and he moved down south several years ago. Me and his wife worked in the same office building, and we sometimes grabbed lunch together during the week. "I'm thinking he could handle all of the landscaping for the property as well. I'd feel better if someone I trusted worked on the grounds, someone who I'd feel safe having around the women who live there."

"Rob's good," he agreed. "And you know him. If he can't do it, though, let me know. I have some contacts that may be able to help."

Tristan always knew somebody. He had an internal rolodex of people who provided various services. His network had assisted me several times.

"How do you know all these people?"

He shrugged. "I just do."

"I guess it's a family trait. I went out with your sisters one day and, I swear, everybody in the restaurant knew at least one of them. Paityn had warned me, but I wasn't prepared. I can only imagine it's worse now."

It wouldn't be a flex if Tristan called his parents celebrities. While they didn't star in movies or write number-one hits, they were well-known in several industries due to their work as marriage and family therapists. They'd published books, separately and together. They'd done TED talks, hosted events, and counseled top-secret clients. And his siblings were right behind them. Many of them had followed in their parents' footsteps, but all of them were successful in their own right.

He finished his beer. "I went to the mall with Asa and Dex while I was home, and all these young women started following us."

"What?" I laughed. "I know you hated that."

He nodded. "I was ready to get the fuck out of there."

"Maybe they read Dexter's book?"

"No," he said. "These women didn't know anything about Dex. It was Asa. Apparently, they'd followed his career, watching his social media, and even joined his gym so they could shoot their shot."

"Wow. It's like that, huh?" I didn't know much about Asa, because he was a lot younger than us, but he definitely had the *fine* trait that Tristan and his brothers had. "He better be careful or someone might catch him."

"I'm not worried. He's young, but he's sensible. Of all my siblings, he's the most like me."

"Unaffected and moody?" I joked.

He squeezed my hand. "Intentional and observant," he corrected. "He's a good guy. I spend the most time with him."

"I didn't know that."

"When we tell my family about us, I'll tell him first."

"Well, Paityn already knows." My friend had called several days ago to discuss what happened. As usual, she'd been nothing but supportive and non-judgmental. Which I'd always appreciated. "We're supposed to go to dinner when she comes to Georgia."

Tristan laughed. "You haven't seen Paityn lately."

I frowned. "Why do you say that? She said she'd be here in a couple of weeks."

He shook his head. "Not going to happen. After her flight back to Cali, the doc and Bishop nixed that when the swelling in her feet didn't go down."

Sucking in a deep breath, I lifted my hand to my chest. "Is she okay?" I knew that Paityn had struggled to conceive, and I'd hoped that her pregnancy would be easy.

"She'll be fine if she sits her ass down somewhere."

My shoulders fell on a sigh. "Well, I'll just have to go see her."

"That's a better plan."

Conversation continued, even after the food arrived. Tristan talked more about his family, signaling he was more comfortable revealing parts of himself. We chatted about religion, about his favorite Sunday school teacher and the time he set an accidental fire in the church vestibule during Vacation Bible School.

"My cousin, Courtney, screamed so damn loud. I thought my world was going to end," he explained.

"How did you start the fire?"

"Stole some firecrackers. I thought I was the shit, showing the kids how to light one. Didn't even think about all the paper in the trashcan."

"Tragic."

"The pact we made not to give each other up fell to the wayside once my father walked into the area. Court gave me up so fast ... I thought I would never see the outside again. I had to apologize to the Pastor, the Deacon Board, the Finance Board, and the Mother Board."

I couldn't imagine Tristan as a kid, standing in front of his church to repent for nearly burning it down. "That's what you get."

"I learned my lesson that day."

"Don't play with fire?"

He met my gaze then. "Nah. I learned that most people—even people you love—will choose to cover their ass first to avoid hard consequences."

I pointed my fork at him. "That's the truth."

"I didn't blame her, though. My dad was not one to play with."

"I bet. So how is Caden related to you?" I'd been to a few family functions and had never seen his cousin before.

"Is he your first cousin?" Tristan pinned me with his intense stare, and I sensed hesitation in his eyes. "We don't have to talk about this," I rushed on, placing my hand on his. "We can move on."

Flipping his hand over, he entwined our fingers, lifted my palm up to his lips, kissed it, then held it against his cheek. The move caught me off guard, and I sucked in a deep breath because it almost seemed like he was using my hand to give him strength in the moment.

"Caden is my biological father's nephew," he said, keeping his voice low. Measured. "I met him when I got expelled from my high school and transferred to another. I was thirteen years old."

"Hm. How did you get expelled?"

"Fighting," he admitted. "I was disrespectful, had a chip on my shoulder. Got into it with a rival and ended up dislocating his jaw. I met Den on my first day. At detention."

"You got put in detention on your first day at a new school?"

"A relative of the guy I fought at my old school cornered me, and I had to show him I wasn't no punk." He averted his eyes, let out a low chuckle. "We bonded over our war wounds. Got to yappin' it up and realized his father was my biological father's younger brother."

Curious, I asked, "Do you have a relationship with that side of your family?"

"Only him. His father was a monster and died young. He was adopted by another family, along with his little brother, Morgan."

"What about your biological father?"

He averted his gaze. "I wanted to meet him, but he refused. Claimed he didn't care to know me. I heard he died a few years ago."

I moved to sit next to him because I just wanted to be close to him, to offer him my strength, my comfort. He didn't pull away, which was encouraging. "I'm sorry, Tristan."

He shook his head. "No need to be sorry. It is what it is."

"Well, it's a good thing you and Caden found each other."

"He's been through a lot. Lost so much. Disappeared for a while, and now he's back. Ready to reclaim his life."

"And you helped him."

He winked. "A little bit."

"Don't discount yourself. You may have had a different start than your siblings, but you are your parents' child."

"You think so?"

"Oh, I *know* so. You helped me. The first time you came to my place and dropped the hint that Paityn was a great friend. I called her and told her about Ashlyn shortly after. You don't get along with Duke, but you were looking out for him the day you met me."

He lowered his head, stared down at our still linked hands.

"Tristan?"

He finally looked at me. "Hey."

I rubbed his chin, brushed my lips over his. "You're going to be okay."

"I want to believe that."

"You will. Everything is a process."

"Look at you, sounding like my parents."

I choked on the water I just sipped. "Listen, if I can be half the professionals they are, I will consider myself successful."

He gripped the back of my head, pulling me into a searing kiss. "I have no doubt."

I leaned back against the chair and patted my stomach. "I'm glad you have faith in me to do my job. Too bad I can't follow my diet. Damn, I ate too much."

Tristan waved the waitress over and settled the bill. Then he stood and pulled me to my feet, kissing me for the entire restaurant to see. "Then, let's get you back to my place. So I can rub your stomach."

I narrowed my eyes. "Is that all you want to rub?"

"Don't tempt me." He kissed the tip of my nose and smoothed his large hand over my butt. "I can think of many things I want to do with my hand ... and my mouth."

We headed out of the restaurant. The buzz of my phone made me pause in place as I fished for it out of my purse. When I found it, I frowned. Five missed calls from Ola. I told Tristan to give me a minute while I dialed Ola.

"Sasha," Ola said, breathlessly.

"Are you okay?" I asked. Tristan walked in front of me, concern shining in his dark eyes. "What's going on?"

"It's Carolyn," she cried. "She's dead."

Chapter Twelve

ZOOM

Tristan

A lie can follow you to death.

The darkness in my heart had consumed me for so long that I surrendered to it, giving it complete control. I'd resigned myself to being alone because I didn't want my poison to affect anyone. The brief glimpses of contentment, the tiny moments of bliss I'd felt could never really overtake it. Most days, I felt like an imposter, destined to live my life in the shadows.

I once thought that Demi could save me, that she could pull me out of my murky existence. But it was Sasha that breathed new life into my lungs, resuscitated me from the depths of despair and anguish. And now it was my turn.

Ashlyn opened the door, tears streaming down her cheeks. "Thanks for coming. I'm so worried about her."

When Ola called to give her the news that Carolyn Fuller died, Sasha's knees had buckled, and I had to carry her out of the restaurant. Instead of taking her to my place, I took her home because I felt she needed to be in her space as she processed her loss.

I stayed with her for a while. Slept on her tiny couch. But this morning, she'd awakened, got dressed, and announced she needed to go to the office. Work had often been therapeutic for me, so I didn't question it. Yet, when Ashlyn called and told me her mother wouldn't talk to her or eat, I heard the fear in her voice and rushed back.

I pointed to the loft area. "Is she up there?"

She shook her head. "On the roof."

Although she had a fear of heights, Sasha wanted to have an outdoor area that could be used for entertainment. Today was the first time I'd heard of her willingly going to her rooftop deck. Mostly, it was used by Ashlyn and her friends.

"I can give you two some space," Ashlyn offered. "I have homework. I'll go to my friend's house." She gripped my wrist. "Please, take care of her."

I hugged her. "I won't let her out of my sight."

"Thanks, Tristan." She climbed into her loft, presumably to get her things.

I cut up an apple and put a few cubes of cheese on a small saucer, then used the hidden steps to go to the patio. Sasha was seated on a small wicker loveseat, a blanket wrapped around her. I walked over to her, raked my gaze over her still form.

"Baby." I rubbed her hair, placed a kiss to the top of her head. "You need to eat." I set the food on the small table. "Just a few bites."

A tear escaped her eye and fell down her cheek. She didn't make a move to wipe it away. "I met Carolyn when I was working as a bartender downtown. She offered me a job that day. And saved my life countless other times. I learned things from her, how to spot a cheater, how to count cards, how to hide money, how to shoot a gun." Her chin trembled. "My relationship with Ashlyn's father was toxic. We fought all day, every day. Physical fights. He was a monster. Abusive. Possessive. He wanted me to quit school, he isolated me from my family. I had just built up the courage to leave him when I found out I was pregnant with Ashlyn. Somehow, she sensed it. I never told her what he'd done to me or anything about him and she knew."

I swallowed past the hard lump that had formed in my throat. I knew all about Carolyn Fuller. I knew that she owned an escort company. I knew that Duke worked for her. I knew that my brother had carried on an affair with the older woman. And I knew that Sasha was connected to him through her.

"She helped me get away from him," Sasha continued. "If it wasn't for her, I would've never been able to escape when I did. That wasn't all. She supported me financially, even after she lost everything. She loved me. And I loved her. I can't believe she's gone."

I wrapped my arms around her, pulling her onto my lap. She sobbed openly, clinging to me, holding on as if I was her lifeline. There were no words, no platitudes, no promised thoughts and prayers. Just us.

Moments later, when her cries had subsided, she whispered, "I saw Duke today."

Frowning, I said, "Really? How is he?"

"Sad." She searched my eyes. "Duke told me you were many things, but not stupid. He said that you probably knew all about Carolyn and that you would never say anything." Another tear fell. "At first, I denied it. I knew that you were good at what you did, but I couldn't believe that you would know about that part of my life and not tell me."

Shame rolled over me as I pondered how to handle this. My instinct was to avoid the conversation, but I couldn't bring myself to do that to her. She deserved the truth. From me. "I knew about Carolyn," I confessed.

Sasha pulled away, and I let her go, already missing the warmth of her body. She went back to her seat, sat up straight. "When did you know?"

"A little while after we met."

"Not from the beginning?"

I shook my head. "Around that time, my family was in crisis. They kept it from me, which wasn't surprising because I hadn't been around in a long time. And you already know what my relationship with my brother is like. Duke left town, then Asa told me a little bit about what was happening. I took it from there."

"So you knew about Ashlyn's father?"

I clenched my teeth as rage intermingled with the desperation I felt in that moment. "I did."

"Why not tell me?"

"What you did to survive is none of my business."

"I worked for her. And not for her HR Consulting Firm."

"It doesn't matter," I whispered. "I don't care what you did to support your family. I just care about you."

She wrapped the blanket around her shoulders. "You do?"

"More than I've ever cared about another woman." The admission was a weight off my shoulders, something that needed to be said while I had the nerve to say it. "Sasha, I meant what I told you. I want *you*. Nobody else. All of your flaws, your experiences, your trauma … it makes you who you are. And *that* woman is the one I want to be with." I held out my hand, hoping she would take it, that she would hold on to it. *To me.*

Time stretched on with me sitting like that, arm outstretched to her. Then she placed her hand in mine and climbed back into my lap. "You have to tell me the truth if this is going to work, Tristan," she said. "I want to be with you, too, but I can't live in the dark anymore. I don't want to be the person I was back then. I want to be free to love you in front of everyone."

Her words, her soft admission made my heart swell. My pulse raced as I struggled to analyze what it all meant. "Sasha, I—"

She placed her hand on my mouth. "Stop. This," she moved my hand to rest it on over her heart, "doesn't need an explanation. I'm not ashamed or unsure. I don't have to quantify it or qualify it. It just is."

Warmth flooded my body, filling the empty spaces of my heart. It had been so long since I'd felt safe, since I'd felt wanted, since I'd felt whole. And I wanted to hold on to the feeling. I needed to hold on to her. "I love you, too," I whispered, wrapping my hand around her neck and kissing her. "I love you, Sasha."

She straddled my lap, returning my kiss with just as much fire. The warmer than normal March breeze swept over my skin, and I took that as a sign. I removed the blanket, dropped it on the floor.

Sasha stared at me as I unbuttoned her blouse and pushed it off her shoulders. I smoothed my hand over her stomach and slipped it under the waistband of her pants. Tracing her slick folds, I pulsed her clit. Her head fell back when I sunk one finger into her heat, then another. I placed wet kisses over her shoulders, over her breasts as I plied her with my fingers. It didn't take her long to come, but when she did, she was stunning. I wanted to bottle this moment, store it in my work bag and take it with me everywhere I went. I wanted to always make her call my name like this. I wanted to dive into her and stay there. *Forever*.

The need to be inside of her was strong, and I turned her over, laying her on her back. I pulled her pants off, kissing my way down her body as she writhed beneath me, begging me to keep going. I tugged her underwear off with my teeth and licked her slit from her clit to her opening, dipping my tongue inside to taste her.

Her low groans, her soft pleas went straight to my dick. But I wasn't done with her. I wasn't finished sampling her.

"Delicious," I murmured against her skin as I ate her, taking my time, bringing her to the brink of her orgasm. "Sasha …" I groaned her name before circling her clit with my tongue and sucking it until she cried out her release. When her trembles subsided, I went in for more, making her come again.

Once I was satisfied, once I had my fill, I made my way back up her body and rested on her. I allowed myself a moment to rake my gaze over her face, lingering on her glassy eyes, her hair fanned out against the cushions of the sofa, her mouth swollen from my kisses. I took in the smell of her skin, the way her mouth lifted into a slight smile. It felt surreal, to give her my heart so freely, to just hand it to her for safe keeping. But I knew it would be fine with her. I knew she'd take care of it.

She pushed my pants down, freeing my dick from its prison. Seconds later, with my eyes locked on hers, I entered her, closing my eyes as sensations spread over me. I was where I was supposed to be. I was home.

We made slow love on the roof of her tiny home, and it was perfect. Two imperfect people coming together, rebuilding and renewing each other with every moment, every kiss. And I was lost in her.

I brushed my lips against her ear. "I love you."

I picked up the pace, alternating between slow and fast movements. She came first, and I pressed my mouth against hers to muffle her cries. My heartbeat pounded in my ears as I came, my own orgasm seeming to crack me open with its intensity. And I surrendered control to it, to her.

Moments later, I heard her voice, whispering that she loved me, that she wanted me. I lifted my head, peered into her eyes. "I love you."

She closed her eyes as a wide smile spread across her lips. "I love you, too. But let's never go this long again."

I sat up, helping her get situated with her back against my chest, then wrapping the blanket around us. I reached over, grabbed the saucer, and held it up. "Please eat."

Groaning, she snatched an apple and bit into it. "We really just made love outside."

"Good thing your neighbors are half a mile away."

She tilted her head up, kissed my chin. "Right? We would've given them a show." She nibbled on another piece of the apple. "Carolyn has no family."

"Yes, she does. You're her family. And Ola."

Nodding, she burrowed into me. "I have to do her justice. Even if no one shows up."

"But you'll be there. And I'll be with you every step of the way."

She sat up, turning to me with wet eyes. "You'd come with me to her funeral?"

"I'll go with you anywhere."

Smiling, Sasha said, "Do you think this is weird?" She bit down on her bottom lip. "We're moving so fast."

"Fifteen years is fast to you?"

She laughed then. "When you put it like that, I guess not."

"As far as I'm concerned, we're a little late."

"Not *too* late." She brushed a finger over my mouth. "Thank you, Tristan."

Words escaped me in that moment because there was so much I still needed to say to her, so much truth that had yet to be told. I wanted this moment to be about her, though. She'd just lost someone important to her and I needed to be her support. As we settled into comfortable silence, wrapped around each other, content with our circumstances, I told myself that we had time to figure everything out.

At least, I hope so.

Chapter Thirteen

LADY IN MY LIFE

Tristan

"*D*o I look okay?"

I smiled as Sasha tugged at her T-shirt, turning in the mirror to check her ass in her blue jeans. Walking up behind her, I wrapped my arms around her waist and placed a gentle kiss on her neck. "You always look good."

She beamed at me. "Thank you." She spun in my arms and wrapped her arms around my neck. "I've heard about your family's softball games. Do I have to play?"

Chuckling, I brushed my thumb over her chin and kissed the tip of her nose. "You're not exactly dressed to play today." I smacked her ass gently, squeezing it in my palm.

Giggling, she shoved me away and unbuttoned her pants. Before she could take them off, I stopped her. "What?" she said. "I have to change."

"You don't have to play. Trust me, my family is way too competitive."

She narrowed her eyes. "And you don't think I can hang?"

Shit. I stared at her, recognizing the mischievous glint in her eyes. Sasha was almost worse than me when it came to wanting to win at every competition. "I know you can, baby," I assured her. "But we're savages on the ball field."

"It's just softball," she said with a shrug. "I used to play a little in high school."

I raised a brow. "A little?" I shook my head. "That's not good enough."

She gaped at me. "Are you seriously trying to play me?"

The start of spring usually meant one thing to my family. Softball. My parents had insisted we all do group activities multiple times per year. The main goal was to get us to work together as a team. When we were younger, we did kickball tournaments. As we grew, we tried bowling, basketball, and flag football. Softball was the one activity we all agreed on, and we'd continued to do it every year. Everyone didn't play, though. There was so many of us, we could alternate on the roster. It was worse now that my siblings were pairing off.

Sasha and Ashlyn had flown to Michigan with me for opening day this year. Our transition from friends-with-benefits to a couple in love had been easy. It seemed like a logical conclusion to invite her to one of our most important family functions.

"I'd never try to play you," I assured her. "How about we just play it by ear? You watch this time and then decide if you want to play."

She pouted. "Whatever."

"You'll be alright." I brushed her cheek with my fore-finger. "You can be my cheerleader."

Sasha scoffed. "Yeah, right. I'll just eat that good popcorn they have at the ballparks." She sighed. "Are you sure we're ready for this?"

After Carolyn died, Sasha went through a period of mourning. Other than Raven, who'd visited a couple of weeks ago, we'd kept our relationship to ourselves. Not that it was a secret either. We were supposed to go live at Paityn's baby shower, but Ashlyn got sick, and Sasha chose to stay in Atlanta with her. Since I didn't particularly care to unscramble baby words and play guessing games, I skipped the event and sent a big gift.

"It's been nice in our little cocoon." She leaned into me. "Warm."

"We can always cancel if you want."

"No, we can't do that. We flew here to be a part of this. I already missed the baby shower."

"You will learn that there are more than enough events to attend. Too many."

"I'll just FaceTime with Paityn while I watch the game."

My sister had given birth a couple of weeks ago. My first nephew, BJ. Bishop Deacon Lang Jr. While I was on an assignment out west, I'd stopped in on them to meet him. The last few weeks of pregnancy were tough for her and Bishop. It was worth getting spit up on to see my sister's smile. Seeing her happy and healthy made me feel better.

"I'm sure you won't be the only one," I said. My sisters talked every day in some capacity. I expected to see Paityn on someone's phone while we were there.

"I love that they're close like that." Against my advice, she changed into a pair of joggers anyway. She held her hands out. "What do you think? Just in case you need to call me in for the save."

I couldn't help but smile at her competitive spirit. "Okay, baby."

"I'm ready. I'll call Ash and tell her to meet us in the lobby." Instead of staying at my small apartment in the city, we decided to rent two hotel rooms—one for us and one for Ashlyn and her friend. Sasha hung up. "They'll be down in five."

The ballpark was packed with teams and their squads preparing to win. My family was hard to miss as they were sitting on a patch of grass away from the crowd. My father was in the middle of the circle, probably giving one of his pep talks. I grabbed Sasha's hand and led them over to them.

Ma spotted us first and her eyes lit up. "You made it."

Raven turned to me. "Dad!" She jumped up and ran into my arms. "I'm glad you made it." She hugged Sasha, then Ashlyn and Cici.

While Raven was in Georgia, she and Sasha had bonded. Although they'd met before, both had made an effort to get to know each other. They found they had several things in common, which helped. Turning her attention to Ashlyn, Raven asked about her recent school project. The two of them had hit it off during her visit, too, and Raven had taken on a sort of mentor role to Ashlyn.

Raven grinned. "Brace yourself," she mumbled.

Sasha leaned in. "Should I be worried?"

"Very," she joked. "Just kidding. You'll be fine. You know us."

Ma made her way over to us, pulling me into a tight hug. "I missed you, son." I held onto her for a moment, enjoying a brief respite in her arms before the deluge of questions. Leaning away, she glanced at Sasha. "Hi, baby." She hugged her. "It's good to see you, too."

"Hi, Mrs. Young." Sasha pulled Ashlyn forward. "I'd like you to meet my daughter, Ashlyn. And her friend Cici."

As Ma bombarded the girls with questions about school, life goals, and young men, I scanned the surprised faces of my family. "What's up? Figured we'd join you today."

Other than Paityn and Duke, everybody was there. Bliss greeted us first, followed by Asa. A slow and steady line formed as they took turns talking to Sasha, Ashlyn, and Cici.

Demi walked up to me. "Hey. How are you?"

It had been a while since I'd seen her. Over the last couple of months, I'd thought about her, but not the way I used to. Instead of awkwardness, though, I felt peace. After everything, I knew that we were both better off. "I'm good."

She smiled. "You look like it." Looking at Sasha, she said, "Hey, girl. Glad you joined us today."

Sasha nodded. "Me too."

When Blake approached us, a smirk on her lips, I squeezed Sasha's hand. No telling what my sister was going to say. "Prayer works, after all." She jabbed my chest with her finger. "You look like you actually might be able to have some fun today, brotha. It'll be an even better day if I finally get my bomb pop."

I groaned. "Get yo' ass out of here with that, B. Lennox, get your wife."

"I'm not his wife yet," she corrected. "I hope he's not this stingy with you, Sasha."

"You're silly." Sasha hugged Blake. "Did you get that referral I sent to you?"

Once Blake and Sasha stepped away for a minute to talk, Asa came back over to me. He glanced at my parents, then at me. "I have a little situation," he muttered under his breath. "I might need your help."

My brother very rarely asked for my help, so I knew something was up. "You good, bruh?"

He shrugged. "To be determined. But I'll get at you later."

Before I could ask more questions, Sasha returned. "Just got a text from Caden." Construction had started on her tiny home community and Den had sent steady updates on the progress. He'd even scheduled several tours of the site so that she could see it in person. "He sent pics. I'll show you later."

"Preston showed me the pics earlier," Dallas chimed in. "What you're doing is pretty amazing. And much needed."

Blake agreed. "I have several clients who may be in the market soon. By the way, you didn't RSVP to the wedding," she said. "Will you be skipping this event too?"

"Is it really going to happen?" I tossed back. Blake had refused to even set a date until recently.

"Shots fired," Asa said, giving me dap.

"Yes, it's going to happen," Bliss added. "If she doesn't cooperate, we'll pull her down the aisle in a red wagon."

Blake stuck her middle finger up. "Fuck all y'all."

Ma held out her palm, signaling it was time for Blake to pay up, which she did begrudgingly.

After my father chastised Blake for making a scene in front of company, he kissed Sasha on her cheek. "I was talking to your baby girl over there. Reminds me of Dallas at that age. Smart as a whip and not afraid to show it. Good job, Mom."

Sasha smiled. "Thank you. That means a lot to me."

Squeezing my shoulder, he said, "I like this look on you, son."

I frowned. "What look is that?"

"Peace." It was amazing how he always knew what I was feeling before I could articulate it. Both he and Ma had that superpower. "I assume you have something to do with this?" he asked Sasha.

Sasha peered up at me, then back at Dad. Before she answered him, I said, "Yes. She has everything to do with this."

"So you're officially together?" Ma asked, hope shining in her eyes. She wrapped her arm around Dad. "Not just here as associates-with-entanglements?"

While my sisters burst out into fits of laughter and Asa just walked away shaking his head, Raven gaped at Ma. "Gram, no. That's not the phrase."

"Where's the lie, though?" Dallas chimed in. "I mean, they're associated with each other through Tyn. And they're in an entanglement." She patted Ma's back. "But just for clarity's sake, it's called friends with benefits."

Ma waved a dismissive hand at my sister. "Oh, hush. I'm trying to get the terminology right. Sasha, Ashlyn, and Cici… welcome to the family. Game time!"

"I need you on short stop today, son," My dad said, bringing us back to the matter at hand. "Are you ladies playing today?"

Ashlyn raised her hand. "I'll play."

"Thank God." Blake kicked her cleats off and handed Ashlyn her glove. "You can take my place. I'd rather do anything else but stand out at center field today."

"No." Bliss sliced a hand through the air. "Not today, Sissy. Ashlyn can take my spot."

I turned to Sasha. "Still think this was a good idea?"

She beamed up at me. "Absolutely."

I rested my forehead on hers and kissed her, freezing when I realized what I'd done. Then, I realized that I didn't give a fuck, so I kissed her again. When I pulled away, Sasha was staring at me with wide eyes. Chuckling, I asked, "What's wrong?"

"I'm not complaining, but you just did that in front of everybody and your Mama."

"Sure did. But I love it," Bliss cooed, clasping her hands against her heart. My little sister loved shit like this. After all, she was a matchmaker by trade. She'd been pulling strings in every sibling relationship since she was a kid. "I love this for you, big brother."

Duke arrived a few minutes later, greeting Demi with a kiss. When he noticed us, he said hello to Sasha. Raven introduced him to Ashlyn and Cici, then he turned to me. "What's up?"

"Nothing," I replied.

The tension between us was still there. We'd seen each other a few times since Dex's wedding, but nothing had changed. Sasha had encouraged me to reach out, but I didn't. Honestly, I didn't know what to say. There was so much that needed to be said, but I wasn't confident a talk would fix things. Still, I knew it had to happen sooner or later.

My father clapped his hands, getting everyone's attention. "Okay, team. It's almost game time. I want that trophy this year."

We all took a seat in a circle as he continued his pep talk. It was more like a string of threats. Needless to say, I wasn't the only one with a competitive streak in the family. As Dad gave everyone their assignments, Sasha leaned over. "Are you okay?"

I met her gaze, nodding slightly. "I'm fine."

"Remember when you said you wanted things to be

different?" She nudged me. "Use this opportunity to do something about it." She kissed me. "Good luck out there. I'm so glad I'm not playing. Your father is intense." Waving at me, she made her way over to the bleachers.

After a rough start, a couple of arguments on the field, and several choice words from Dad—and Ma—the team won both games. Every year, whether we won or lost, my parents hosted an opening day feast at the house. Usually, I skipped it, but Ashlyn wanted to go so we went.

As we ate dinner, I thought about the day. We'd done what we set out to do, and it didn't break us. Sasha and Ashlyn felt at home, Raven was happy, and I wasn't looking for an escape. All in all, it was a success.

"I had so much fun today." Sasha looped her arm through mine as we walked the grounds of my parents' estate. "I haven't laughed that much in a long time."

"That was my bright spot." We took a seat on the boat launch. "Seeing you happy."

"I am. Makes me miss my siblings." Since I'd known her, she hadn't spent a significant amount of time with her brothers or her sister. I knew that had a lot to do with their past, the trauma they'd experienced growing up with their father.

"We're all so spread out and focused on our own lives," she continued. "Being here with your family lit a fire under me, though. It's not enough to just talk on the phone every now and then. Face time is important."

A few months ago, I would've disagreed. In my mind, it was okay to keep a distance. Yet, there was something about seeing my own family through someone else's eyes. Watching Raven and Ashlyn together, seeing Sasha with Ma was all the proof I needed to know that it was time for me to get my head out of my own ass. My family had welcomed them, no questions asked. Once anyone was part of this family, they were always part of the family. That included me.

"I used to wonder what my life would've been like if Sheila hadn't given me away," I whispered. Up until that point, I hadn't talked about my biological mother to Sasha, and she hadn't pushed. "Would I be me?"

"I think you would've been a version of you. Definitely not the same."

"I hated her for so long."

She slipped her arm around me, squeezing me gently. "That's understandable."

"My parents thought they were doing the right thing by giving me her journals, but reading her true thoughts about life, about me … broke me." My throat burned as tears threatened to fall. "I couldn't reconcile how she felt about me with how Ma did. I didn't understand how someone who didn't give birth to me could really love me when my own mother resented my existence. So I was always waiting for Ma to admit she never cared about me."

"She'll never admit that because it's not true." She tilted her head to meet my gaze. "Your mother is Victoria Young. Having contractions and labor pains doesn't make that any less true."

Swallowing rapidly, I continued, "In hindsight, I can see that Sheila was a sick woman. She didn't even know how to love herself."

"Which makes her decision the right one. She gave you to someone who could give you everything she couldn't. I don't know … sounds like love to me."

Dad always told me that love was a verb, not an empty platitude. Love was hard work, commitment, understanding, and consistency. It was intentional. It was time management. It was the hard truth even when it doesn't feel good. *Even if I can lose everything by telling it.* I'd seen it in action through the way they loved us and each other. *I want it for myself.*

"It does, doesn't it?" I said into the night air. Sheila loved me in her own way. She'd given me the best gift—parents who rose to the challenge, two people who'd shown me every day that I was wanted. After all these years, I felt secure in that.

Then, the dam broke. I dropped my head as the tears fell, as my heart finally accepted what I'd been afraid to believe. I cried for Sheila, for my parents, for my siblings, and for myself. I'd held it in for so long, I wondered if the tears would ever stop flowing. It seemed like each tear represented my internal walls coming down and being rebuilt. Instead of feeling weak, I felt stronger. And when the tears subsided, Sasha was there, holding me up, offering me a lifeline.

I kissed her brow. "Thank you."

She wiped my cheeks. "You don't have to thank me, Tristan. You can always lean on me. I promise I won't break."

I smiled. "Good to know."

We sat there for a few minutes, enjoying the silence. After a while, she gasped. "Oh my goodness."

"What?" I scanned the area around us, wondering if she'd seen someone or something.

"Asa probably ate all that banana pudding. I didn't even get a taste."

I cracked up. "You should probably get on that because he's been known to steal the whole pan." I stood and held out a hand. She slipped hers in mine, and I helped her up. "Save me some, too. For later."

We started back toward the house but stopped when I saw Duke walking toward us. He stopped in front of me. "We need to talk."

Sasha let out a deep breath. "I'll see you inside."

Once she was out of sight, I looked at Duke. "What's up?"

"Shit, I don't know." He rubbed the back of his head. "This is harder than I thought it would be." He leaned against the rail. "I fell in love with a woman who calls me on my bullshit every single day."

I laughed. "Me too. But they're usually right."

He eyed me curiously. "I haven't been fair to you."

Staring out at the water, I nodded. "I could say the same thing to you."

"I was angry that you shit on our relationship when I should've tried to understand where you were coming from. The whole Aunt Sheila thing … That was fucked up. You were just a kid struggling to process difficult emotions."

It was the same thing Sasha said. It made sense that Duke had echoed the sentiment because he was smart like that. He was the most like Dad. I hated him for it then. Now, I understood what a burden that may have been for him.

Sighing, I said, "still no excuse." Last year, my brothers and sisters had cared enough to tell me how wrong I was. I wasn't strong enough to hear it then, but they were right. "I shouldn't have taken it out on you or anyone else."

"That night, when Demi showed up on our doorstep, something in me shifted. I didn't recognize it at the time. I just knew that I had to protect her no matter what. Even from you. *Especially* from you."

"You weren't wrong," I admitted. "That night, I realized that you were the best person to protect her. I resented you for it because you know I'm competitive like that. I'm not proud of how I acted, how I treated Demi, or how I treated you. I told you to take care of her, but my need to win eclipsed what I knew was right. I'm sorry." Without even thinking about it, I hugged him. A quick man hug, but it was a step in the right direction.

"I'm sorry, too, bruh." He cleared his throat. "But that's enough of this emotional shit."

Chuckling, I agreed. "It was a long time coming, though."

He smirked. "You and Sasha, huh?"

"Yeah. Me and Sasha."

"When did that start?"

"A long time ago." I told him about the first time I'd seen her at Bar Louie with him. Curiosity had led me to her apartment and the rest was history.

Duke swallowed visibly. "Sasha's a good woman. Strong."

He didn't have to tell me that. I saw the strength in her eyes every day. "She's been through a lot."

"You knew about Carolyn?"

I nodded. "I found out shortly after you left town. One of my regrets was that I didn't push my feelings aside to be there for you. As your big brother."

"That would've been nice." He tossed a rock into the lake. "I'm someone's father."

My eyes flashed to his. "What?"

"Carolyn had my son while I was overseas and gave him up for adoption."

The pieces were coming together. Sasha, when she returned from work. The despair she felt. "Did Sasha know?"

"She told me the day after Carolyn died. Don't be mad at her."

I wasn't angry that she didn't tell me. Sasha was a vault. She didn't share anyone's secrets. And I preferred it that way. "I'm not."

"Yeah, you wouldn't be."

"Does the family know?"

"Just X and Demi. I'm not even sure how or when to tell everyone else."

"Have you tried to find him?"

"I know where he is." He peered up at the sky. "I went to him, with every intention of telling him I was his father. But then I saw him with his mother. He was loved, happy. I couldn't take that away from him."

Duke's words resonated with me in a way that I couldn't quite describe. He'd been robbed of time with his son, yet he loved him enough to put him first. The situation mirrored mine in so many ways, except Sheila was Duke in this scenario.

"Strangely enough, you were one of the first people I wanted to tell."

His admission caught me off guard. "I'm glad you told me today. I won't say anything."

"I know." He tapped the railing with his thumb, before shifting his gaze to me. "I always knew that."

"For what it's worth, your son is lucky to have a parent who put his needs first."

"I had no choice. I am Mom and Dad's son. And so are you."

My heart clenched in my chest as fresh tears burned the back of my throat. "Right."

Duke and I had turned a corner that night. We found common ground in the unlikeliest of places, in our past and with the women we chose to love. And we were still brothers—no matter what.

Chapter Fourteen

NO ORDINARY LOVE

Sasha

Summer had ushered in a new season of possibilities. Three women had leased lots in my development, Ashlyn had been accepted in a study abroad program for high school seniors, and I was happier than I'd ever been. Tristan played a huge role in that.

Initially, I wasn't sure how my life would change once I chose to love Tristan, once we decided to do this. We'd been part of each other's lives for so long, it didn't seem like a huge shift. The moments we'd shared over the last several months, the glimpses of him that he'd revealed, were everything.

Of course, there were some hiccups. Like my house. Ashlyn was right. Tristan was too big for my tiny home. So we'd improvised. We agreed that we wouldn't move in together until Ashlyn graduated from high school next year, but he'd purchased an RV and parked it on the lot next to mine. That allowed us a chance to spend most evenings together.

While our relationship had grown so much in a short period of time, Ashlyn and Tristan had bonded more as well. They were so cute together, watching old documentaries for fun and playing video games. I had no idea that I was in love with a gamer. Tristan was hard core, and Ashlyn was all in because she loved video games, too.

Currently, they were downstairs playing some horror game together. We'd flown to Michigan for Blake's wedding and decided to rent a house instead of a hotel this time. Tristan wasn't wrong about his family. Every month, there was something going on. It was overwhelming, and we'd skipped several events, but we'd shown up quite a bit, too. Especially since a few of his family members had made Atlanta their home, including Raven, who'd moved down south after she graduated from college to work for Chef Duke.

Speaking of Duke, the brothers continued to work through their issues. Don't get me wrong, they still clashed, but they also didn't let too much time pass before they talked it out.

"Baby!" Tristan called. "You ready yet?"

I heard Ashlyn scream at the television and smiled to myself. "In a minute." I put my earrings in and spun around in the mirror one last time before making my way downstairs. "Ready. How do I look?"

Tristan's eyes raked over my body slowly. His gaze was like a soft caress, and my skin tingled as if he'd touched me with his hands. Or his tongue. "You look good," he said.

"Thanks, baby." I bent down to kiss him. "Let's go."

Ashlyn turned the game off. "I'm a little nervous. I don't know anyone."

"That's why we're going," I explained. "I want you to get to know your uncles and your aunt."

Tonight, we were going to my brother Nero's house. He'd invited us over to meet his new girlfriend, Daphne. But I wasn't the only one he'd invited. Vincent and Josslyn would be there. Leah and Junior had arrived yesterday and planned to join us, too. It had been years since we were all in the same room together, and I couldn't wait to see my siblings.

The drive to Detroit seemed longer than usual, probably because my nerves were bad. But when we got there, when I saw my siblings, I felt like I was transported back in time to when life wasn't that bad, and our biggest problem was who controlled the television on Saturday mornings.

Josslyn hugged me for the fifth time. "I missed you, Sasha."

I wiped tears from her cheeks. "Same. We have to do better."

"I know."

Vincent rested his head on top of mine. "This was a great idea, Nero. You just don't know how much I needed this." My brother had changed so much from the skinny kid who used to breakdance on the kitchen floor. But he'd done quite well for himself. Like Nero, he was a physician, working for a small hospital in California. He never had any children of his own, but he'd adopted his wife's son.

I squeezed his wrist. "I agree. We should definitely do this once a year."

Nero poured me another glass of wine. "We can alternate destinations." He pointed behind me. "Look at them."

I glanced over at Ashlyn, who was talking animatedly with her cousins. Nero had two daughters who were just as intelligent as Nero. My brother's grandfather was a pillar in the Black community, and he'd grown up an activist. Even now, he put in countless hours volunteering at a clinic, teaching, and advocating for those who didn't have fair access to health treatment. Earlier, Ashlyn was riveted as they'd talked about their volunteer work. And she'd begged to come back and attend an event on campus in the fall. It was good seeing her making connections with family. Mine and Tristan's.

"I love it," I mused. "She was so nervous before she came."

"She'll be alright," Nero assured me.

I watched as Junior and Ashlyn started teaching my nieces the latest TikTok dance. "I wish Shaun was here to see this," I said, swallowing past a lump in my throat. "I miss him."

"Junior looks just like him." Josslyn wiped a tear from her face. "I couldn't believe it when I saw him walk in that door. Took me back to the block, watching him play ball at the park. I keep imagining what he'd be like today."

Leah sniffed. "He would've been the loudest one in here."

"And eating all the food," Vincent added.

"Talking all that shit," Nero said. "I would've gladly took his money on the card table."

"That's right." Josslyn scooped a mound of salsa onto a small plate. "How's Ola?" she asked.

Ola had moved to Georgia when Carolyn died. She worked part time at a nursing home. "She's doing good. Still bossy."

Leah snorted. "Always trying to tell me what to do." She shrugged. "I live in a whole other state. Married with kids, but she still calls to see if I cooked vegetables for dinner."

Cracking up, I bumped her hip. "That's love right

there. If it wasn't for those green beans she made every night, we wouldn't have had anything healthy to eat."

Daphne breezed in from the kitchen, a tray of chicken wings in her hand. She set them on the table. "Dinner is almost ready."

When we'd arrived earlier, Daphne had been more than gracious to us. She'd entertained us with the story of how she and Nero ended up together. Apparently, she'd cussed him out via text, only to realize she'd sent the text to the wrong person. Much to my brother's benefit, though, because he'd taken his shot that day. And now they were combining homes.

The doorbell rang just as we sat down to eat. Daphne rushed to the front of the house. I turned to Tristan, who'd been talking sports with Josslyn's boyfriend. "This is better than I imagined," I whispered. "I'm glad you're with me."

He kissed the inside of my wrist. "I wouldn't be anywhere else."

Daphne strolled back into the room, followed by a woman. "Y'all, this is my best friend, Britt."

Tristan stiffened next to me.

I looked at him. "What's wrong?"

"Nothing," he said.

I watched as Nero went down the line, calling out each of our names. When he got to me, Britt paused, but covered quickly by holding out her hand. I shook hers, noticing the way her gaze shifted to Tristan.

Interesting.

As we ate, I pondered how the two of them were connected. It was obvious they knew each other. Yet, unlike how he'd acted at his parents' house back in the day with me, he seemed content to act like he'd never seen her before. That alone gave me pause because it just wasn't like him.

After dinner, we settled into their sunroom for drinks and conversation. My nieces took Ashlyn and the others to the bowling alley. I enjoyed hanging out, learning about my siblings' lives, but I wasn't fully immersed in the discussion because my mind was on Tristan. He was present, but the walls we'd broken down were there again.

I glanced at Britt across the room. The woman looked regular enough, definitely not an IG model. She was dressed down, shorts and a T-shirt. Her hair was styled in boho braids. *Regular*. She was talking to Daphne, but every so often, her eyes would drift over to me. *Do I know her?*

Nero brought out the cards, per Vincent's request, and we started a game of Spades. Tristan and I were up first, but something was off. Tristan couldn't meet my gaze for longer than a few seconds at a time. As a result, we lost quick because we weren't in sync. It bothered me, and I wanted to confront him. But I wouldn't do it there in front of everyone.

When Tristan excused himself, Leah leaned over and whispered, "What's wrong with him?"

"I don't know." I glanced at Britt, only to find her looking at me again. "But I'm going to find out."

"He's being weird."

"Do you know that woman? Britt?"

Leah shrugged. "No. Why?"

I folded my arms over my breasts and stared at her, silently letting her know that she could try me if she wanted to. She didn't avert her gaze either. "No reason," I whispered.

An hour later, I went into the house looking for Tristan. Drinks were flowing and the music was blasting. It was a good time. And I wished I could enjoy it, but I needed to settle something. Now.

I found Tristan outside, standing near the truck we'd

rented. He was peering at his phone, engrossed in his screen. "Hey," I said, approaching him.

He lifted his eyes. "Hi."

Hugging myself, I leaned against the truck. "What's going on, Tristan?"

His shoulders fell. "Why do you ask?"

"Because I know you. When Britt came, you left. Do you know her?"

Glancing at me out of the corner of his eye, he said, "Yes."

My stomach roiled and I waited for him to elaborate. But when he didn't say anything else, I asked, "Come on, now. Don't play me. How do you know her?"

"We hooked up a time or two," he admitted softly.

"Is that it?"

Tristan shifted, turning to face me. "Sasha, there's something—"

"Well ..." Britt strolled out to us, fury in her eyes. "Funny running into you here after all these years, Tristan."

This bitch. "Who the hell do you think you are?" I shouted, not even caring that we were in the middle of a residential neighborhood. A nice one at that. "And why do you think it's okay to just come out here and interrupt my conversation with my man?"

"I have business with *your* man."

I didn't like the way she'd emphasized that Tristan was *my* man. It almost felt like she was taunting me. It knocked me off my square, and I wanted to beat the shit out of her for it. "Look, I don't know who you are, but don't go there with me."

"Really? Did he tell you how he knows me?"

"Britt," Tristan warned, his voice low.

I'd never heard him talk to a woman like that before.

I'd only ever heard that tone one time. And that was when a guy at the bar wouldn't take no for an answer. We'd just started seeing each other casually, and he'd met me for drinks at Bar Louie. One of my regular patrons had too much to drink and kept asking me out. Tristan had told him to leave me alone, but Old Man Taylor kept teasing. Until Tristan stood from his seat.

"We met at a friend's barbecue," she said, ignoring him and addressing me. "We hooked up that night."

"Okay." I shrugged. "He already told me that. And?"

"I offered him a job, and—"

"You need to leave," Tristan interrupted. "Now."

Rolling her eyes, she continued, "It's kind of funny how he's with you. I wonder how you met."

"It doesn't matter," I told her. "Our relationship is none of your business."

"But it is," she insisted. "You know Marlon Ware?"

Dread. I felt it as it traveled through my body, from my head to my feet. Because I knew Marlon, alright. He was Ashlyn's father. I blew out a deep breath, counted to ten. "Who are you?"

"I'm someone who had a vested interest in ensuring that Marlon never hurt anyone else again."

Tristan's hand on my back startled me, and I jerked away from him, glaring at him. "Don't touch me."

"Sasha, wait."

I whirled around and pointed at Britt. "Who are you?" I repeated. "How do you know Marlon?"

"He killed my husband and left me to raise our son by myself." She turned to Tristan. "I went to Tristan and asked him to find him because I had reason to believe that he faked his death. You were in the picture I showed him. I found it in my husband's belongings."

I sucked in a deep breath, bracing myself on the car

behind me. I felt like my knees were going to give out. Because if what she was saying was true, if what she was implying was …

"Tristan," I breathed, "you better tell me the truth."

Britt snickered. "He—"

Holding up my hand, I yelled, "Stop. I want to hear it from him. You can leave now."

She seemed to accept that and backed up. "Just thought you should know." Then, she pivoted on her heels and walked into the house.

"Sasha, please," Tristan whispered.

"Please what? Believe you? How am I supposed to believe you when you haven't said anything yet?"

Tristan pounded his fist on the hood of the truck, the loud boom echoing in the night air. "Britt wanted me to find Marlon."

"He's dead," I growled.

"She didn't think so," he explained. "She came to me and told me that word on the street was that he might be alive and hiding out."

The thought was inconceivable. Because if Marlon was alive, there was no way he wouldn't have come for me, for his daughter. "He's dead," I spat out, cursing the angry tears that fell. "That nigga is gone. And you fucked up."

"I didn't take the job."

"But I wasn't exactly a stranger to you when you came up to me at that bar, right?"

I dropped his head. "Right."

"So it wasn't about Duke or the fact that you saw me with him?"

"I didn't lie to you about that. I went to Bar Louie because I remembered your picture from Paityn's social media. I was curious. And very concerned that my sister was hanging out with someone who was connected to a murderer. I needed to meet you, to see if you had any idea who you were with. Then, I saw you with Duke. In my mind, that was enough to walk in that bar. Once I met you, though, I decided not to take the job."

His reasoning was sound. And if he had told me that from the beginning, maybe I would've accepted it. But now it just felt like betrayal. It made me question everything between us. "You came to my house."

"I did." He grabbed my hand. "And I saw Ashlyn, just like I told you."

"Why didn't you just say something?" I smacked his chest. "Why would you keep that from me? Especially knowing how evil that man was. What if he was still alive? Don't you think I should've known?"

"After I met you, I searched for him. I looked everywhere, turned over every rock. I called in favors. I didn't find anything. A friend of mine in the police department didn't turn up anything either. So I just chalked it up to Britt being a grieving widow angry that her husband was taken away from her."

I was so pissed I hadn't realized I was crying until he brushed my tears away. I swatted his hand. "Don't touch me." I paced back and forth, unable to think, unable to process what had just happened. "I need to leave." She tapped at her phone furiously.

"Sasha, let me take you home."

A couple of minutes later, Leah rushed out of the house. "What the hell did you do?" She glared at me. "I told yo' muthafuckin' ass to watch your step." She tilted her head, brushed my hair out of my face. "Sis, let's go."

"Sasha, wait," he called.

But it was too late. Leah walked me to her rental, opened the door, and waited until I was inside before she closed the door. I heard her yelling at Tristan. "You better be glad Ashlyn is not here. I don't want her to see her like this, so you need to take your Black ass somewhere else tonight."

After we left Tristan standing in the middle of the street, I called my brother to let him know that I got sick. I assured him that I was fine and that I would see them all before we left town. Leah stopped for treats, and I was currently cookie wasted, splayed out on the sofa at my Airbnb.

"I just can't believe this." I buried my face in my hands. "How could he lie to me like that?" I'd told Leah everything, starting with Britt and ending with that confrontation outside. All I needed now was for her to tell me I was right. Except, she didn't say anything. Twisting my head around, I asked, "Leah. Say something."

Leah sighed. "It's not going to be what you want to hear."

"What is it?"

"Sis, not saying he was right, but Tristan didn't take the job."

"It doesn't matter," I snapped.

"Actually, it does. He told you that he approached you out of concern for his sibling. It just happened to be Paityn *and* Duke. He didn't lie when he told you that finding out you were a mother had changed things for him because it did. And that was after he didn't take the job."

"But he lied."

"By omission. Back in the day, we did that all the time. You said yourself that you lied to survive. Many times. Yes, he should've told you long before now. But I find it hard to believe that he did it maliciously. I can see that he loves you so much. I saw it then. He's proven it every day."

As Leah spoke, I knew she was telling the truth. Tristan

never claimed to be perfect. He'd always said he'd done things he regretted. Still … "He acted like he knew nothing about Myron."

"Shit, I don't want to know anything about that mutha-fucka either. He told you he tried to find any proof that he was alive. I don't think he would've put forth the effort it if wasn't for you."

"Like you said, he was protecting his siblings."

"But when he realized that Marlon was dead … Why stick around? Why maintain contact?"

"Because I was easy," I muttered lamely.

She barked out a laugh. "Girl, please. I've been around Tristan for years. He doesn't strike me as the type of man that goes for easy." Scooting forward, she grabbed my hand. "Sis, you can be mad tonight. You can eat all these damn cookies and be bloated in the morning. But tomorrow you're going to get your head out of your ass and go talk to him."

"I—"

"No. I've never seen you as happy as you've been the last several months. Ashlyn loves him. You love him. This isn't insurmountable. Do what you tell your clients. Work it out."

Chapter Fifteen

BEFORE I LET YOU GO

Tristan

"Here."

I grabbed the bottle of water Den had handed me. "Thanks."

Den had been in town for business and was using my old apartment. "Sorry about earlier."

When I'd arrived at my place, I nearly lost an eye when he emerged from the bedroom, gun in hand, ready to shoot thinking I was an intruder. I'd dived on the floor, injuring myself because I landed wrong. "No problem," I grunted, massaging the small of my back. "I should've called."

"Good thing I didn't bring that waitress home tonight."

I shifted, relieving some of the pressure on my back. "That would've been unfortunate."

"Why are you here, though?"

"Sasha didn't want me to go back to the rental."

He frowned. "What happened?"

"It's over."

The moment Britt had arrived earlier, I knew that I was on borrowed time. Even now, I turned over every detail in my mind, pondered all the various outcomes. And it was simple. *I fucked up*. There were so many opportunities to tell her the whole truth, not just parts of it. And I'd failed every time. Then, as we fell into the relationship, as we grew closer, I got comfortable in it. I told myself that it was an insignificant piece to the puzzle.

"I betrayed her trust," I said. "No telling if I'll ever get it back."

Den took a sip from his bottle of water. "It can't be that bad. Sasha is reasonable. Can't you work it out?"

"I think she just needs time."

"What if she doesn't?" Den asked. "What if she just needs you to get off your ass and fight for her?"

"I can't make her talk to me."

"Maybe not, but you can talk to her. I know you, bruh. I can envision the scene. She yelled. You stood there like a rock. That's you. All day."

"You don't know what you're talking about," I argued. "I talked." *A little*.

"What did you say?"

I can't remember. Nothing much. "Shut the hell up, man."

"You already know you fucked up. You should've been honest with her from jump. I don't know why you withheld that information."

In hindsight, I didn't know either. Sasha had pegged me right from the beginning. I was a desperate mutha-fucka. I could've told her. I didn't because I didn't want *this* to happen. I didn't want to lose her.

Den shook his head. "Look, I spent a lot of years

running from myself. I lost everything that I loved. My girl, my brothers … Because I was a dumb ass."

A while ago, Den was engaged to be married, ready to walk down the aisle, when his fiancée found out he'd been cheating on her. He'd made questionable choices throughout their relationship, squandered every chance she'd given him to get himself together. Now she was happily married to someone else—his brother.

Sydney was to Den what Demi was to me. She was his redemption arc. Much like I'd done, he'd held on to her even as he continued to hurt her. I didn't want to repeat the same cycle with Sasha. If she really didn't want to be with me, I would have to let her go.

Even if it destroys me.

Den stood. "Don't be like me." Then he disappeared into the bedroom.

I tossed and turned all night, but when I awoke the next morning, I knew what I had to do. Today was Blake's wedding, but I needed to talk to Sasha before I went. I drove over to the rental, expecting to see Leah's car out front. There were lights on, so I let myself in.

The house was quiet. I walked into the kitchen, hoping she'd be there fixing breakfast. She was an early riser and liked to eat before nine. The kitchen was empty. I walked upstairs to the master bedroom. She wasn't there.

I dialed her number, and it went straight to voicemail. "Shit," I grumbled.

"Tristan?" Ashlyn poked her head inside.

"Hey, Ash." I forced a smile on my face. "Good morning."

"Are you looking for Mom?"

Unsure what Sasha had told her, I chose to act like everything was good between us. "Do you know where she went?"

Yawning, she stretched. "She left with Leah. Something about breakfast with Uncle Nero and everybody."

"Oh."

Ashlyn wiped her eyes. "Are you two fighting?"

I blinked. "Huh?"

"You weren't here last night. She told me you were with your family, but it just felt weird."

Closing my eyes, I sat down on the bed. "We had a disagreement," I admitted.

She walked into the room and sat down next to me. "What happened? Are you two going to break up?"

As smart as Ashlyn was, as mature as she'd always been, right now she looked like a little girl. Scared that her world was going to be rocked. Again. But I got myself into this by not being honest, so I told her the truth. "I hope not."

"She's mad at you?"

I nodded. "I messed up." I wouldn't go into specifics with her, but I wanted to be upfront. "I hurt your mom. I didn't mean to, though. I told myself I was doing the right thing, protecting her. And you."

"Like you've always done?"

Ashlyn wasn't my daughter, but I loved her like she was. When I imagined my future, I envisioned walking Ashlyn down the aisle when she was ready to get married or playing video games with her kids. *My grandkids.* "Like I've always *tried* to do."

"You didn't just try, Tristan. You've been the only father figure I've ever had. I used to be so jealous of my friends who knew their fathers. Then, I realized I didn't have it that bad. I had you."

My heart swelled in my chest from her soft admission. When I made up my mind to fight for Sasha, I was fighting for Ashlyn, too. I was fighting to hold on to the life we'd built together. I held her hand. "Thanks, Ash. That means the world to me. *You* mean the world to me."

She hugged me. "I love you, Tristan."

"Love you, too." I rubbed her back, willing myself to hold it together. The last thing I wanted to do was cry in front of Ashlyn.

But when she pulled back, she wiped a tear that I didn't know had fallen. "There. All clear. So, I think we're still coming to the wedding."

Hope surged in my chest. "Is that what she said?"

"No, but I plan to make it hard for her to say no."

"Have you been talking Bliss?"

Ashlyn grinned. "Sometimes. We video chat every now and then."

My sister had stepped into the role of aunt so seamlessly that I knew I had to make it official sooner than later. "Make sure you stay away from Blake, though," I joked.

"I love Auntie B. She tells it like it is. She helped me get rid of this boy I met at school. He just kept asking me to the movies. I can't stand him. She told me exactly what to say to him. She—"

I held my hand up. "I don't need to know," I said. "I know my sister. And it probably wasn't nice."

"It definitely wasn't," she confirmed.

"And who is this guy?"

She waved a dismissive hand my way. "Nobody now," she chirped.

I kissed her brow. "Good. I'm going to head to Ann Arbor. Call me if I need to come back."

"You won't. I got this."

"Then I'm in good hands."

Ashlyn hugged me again. "See you later."

Later, I stood at the entrance to the church waiting for Sasha. I stared at the last text Ashlyn had sent.

Ash: **She's still not home.**

That was over an hour ago. My calls to Sasha went unanswered and Ashlyn had yet to text me back with an update. But I waited because the alternative was too hard to consider.

Before I could dial Sasha again, though, I spotted someone familiar out of the corner of my eye. The bride. Blake was walking down the street in her wedding dress.

Bliss burst through the door and pointed. "There she is."

One by one, all of my siblings raced down the street toward Blake. Of course, I had no choice but the follow. To make sure they weren't having too much fun. When I approached them, they were all huddled around Blake. And she was crying.

"Sissy, it's okay." Paityn's soft voice spread a bit of calm over the situation. "What's wrong?"

Blake shrugged. "This doesn't feel right to me."

"Why?" Dallas asked. "Are you and Lennox fighting?"

Shaking her head, she said, "No. It's this." She gestured to her dress and pointed to the church. "All of this. I don't want to do this."

"Do you want to marry Lennox, B?" Duke asked.

"Of course I do," she snapped. "I want to be with him more than anything."

Dex rubbed her back. "But you said this doesn't feel right."

"It feels like it's not us," she admitted. "The church, the spectacle. When I envisioned my wedding, I only saw us. On a beach somewhere or in the mountains. No one around to see it because it's personal. It's between me and him."

"So why did I have to buy a tuxedo then?" Asa asked.

"Right," Duke agreed. "You could've saved a lot of

time and money if you'd just said that shit a long time ago."

Blake sniffed. "I should've followed my first mind. I just got caught up in the pomp and circumstance, Mom's excitement at picking out my dress, and Dad's pride when he talked about walking me down the aisle."

Paityn and Dallas had married in unconventional ways. Paityn had eloped for her first marriage and then had a backyard wedding when she married Bishop. A very pregnant Dallas went to the courthouse a week or two before her scheduled delivery.

"I never thought I'd be the first daughter to have all of this," Blake exclaimed. "I assumed it would be Bliss."

Bliss hugged Blake. Up until that point, she'd been pretty quiet, letting everyone else talk. But it was obvious that Blake needed to hear from her twin sister.

"Sissy," Bliss said, "I'm sorry if I pressured you to do this. I heard what you didn't say. You talked about Mom and Dad, but I've been in your ear, pushing you along. I guess I was just living a little through you. But if this doesn't feel right to you, I don't want you to do it."

Looking at me, Blake asked, "What do you think?"

It felt like a moment of truth. For once, my baby sister was asking for my advice, my counsel. And I planned to rise to the occasion. I scanned their faces quickly before locking my gaze on Blake. "I'm sorry for not being a better big brother. To all of you." I grabbed her hand. "Sasha told me it was never too late, though, so I'm ready to step up today. Say the word and I'll take your ass up out of this church and dare *anyone* to say something to you."

Dallas shrugged. "This what they gotta know."

We all laughed at that phrase. Which was basically another way of saying "*try me if you want to*."

"Uh oh," Asa murmured.

I turned around to find Lennox approaching us tentatively. "What's going on?" He cut in between us, making a beeline straight to Blake. "Baby, what's wrong?"

Blake looked at me, and I gave her a nod. Then, she peered up at Lennox. "I want to be your wife, Lennox. But I don't want to do it here."

Lennox frowned. "Why didn't you just tell me?"

His words brought me back to Sasha. *Why didn't I just tell her?* I checked my phone again. No missed calls. No texts.

"Because I didn't want to hurt anyone," Blake replied.

I never wanted to hurt her.

"I'm not hurt," Lennox said. "I don't care if we get married here or on someone's farm. You could wear jeans or nothing at all. I just want to be your husband. I want a life with you."

Blake hugged Lennox, kissing him as the tears streamed down her face. When they pulled apart, she said, "How are we supposed to get out of here?"

I pointed to the Ford Expedition I'd rented. "Truck is over there." I tossed Lennox the keys. "Dallas will give y'all's regrets."

Dallas gaped. "Me? You're the oldest.

"You always say you're the boss," Asa chimed in. "You should do it."

"No!" she argued, glancing at Paityn. "You can—"

"Nope." Paityn lifted her hands up. "I have to go feed the baby. You can tell Mom and Dad, too."

Dallas' shoulders slumped. "Y'all are fucked up for this. Duke? Dex?"

I squeezed her shoulders. "It's okay. I'll take care of Mom and Dad. You can make the announcement to the church."

"I'll do it," Bliss said. "Lennox, you need to bring one of your sisters in on this before you leave."

Lennox nodded. "I'll text Dana to come out."

Plan in place, we headed back to the church. Ma was standing at the door, hands on her hips and *that* look in her eyes. She was pissed. Everybody brushed past her, kissing her as they hurried into the church, leaving me behind.

"Tristan," Ma said. "What is going on? Where is Blake?"

"Is Dad around?"

Ma closed her eyes, letting out a deep sigh. "She ran, didn't she? Hold on. Let's go find him."

Dad was in the pastor's study, reading his Bible. When we walked into the room, he smiled at Ma. "Hey, beautiful. You're stunning."

"Brace yourself," she told him, motioning to me. "Go ahead, Tristan."

They never beat around the bush, so I didn't either. "Blake's not getting married today."

Nodding, Dad hummed a little tune. I recognized it immediately as one of his favorite hymnals, "Great is Thy Faithfulness." A moment passed before he finally stood. "Okay. I can take this suit off now."

"Baby," Ma said. "Did you hear him?"

"I did." Dad kissed Ma. "Vee, you know we can't force it. Blake has the final say."

"Fine. Wait 'til I see that girl, though." She stomped to the door, fussing along the way.

"Wait, Ma," I said, stopping her before she could leave. "Can I talk to you?"

Ma paused, turning to me. "Is it something good or bad? Just so you know, I will not be held liable for what comes out of my mouth right now."

I laughed, squeezing her hand and leading her over to the chair she'd just vacated. "It's not bad."

"But it's not good either," she said, folding her arms over her chest.

Unbothered, Dad leaned back in his chair, crossing one leg over his knee. "What's up, son?"

"I feel like I need to say something to both of you. Something I should've said a long time ago."

Ma's scowl softened. A little. "Are you okay? Are you sick?"

"No. But I *am* sorry." Taking a seat across from them, I leaned forward, resting my elbows on my knees, "I realize now that you did the best you could under the circumstances. I put you through a lot. I didn't know how to handle my emotions, and I took it out on you when all you've ever done was love me."

Dad placed his handkerchief in Ma's palm, and she dabbed at her eyes.

"Can you please forgive me?" I pleaded.

"Oh, son. Get up." She stood up, holding her arms out. "Already done."

I walked into her embrace. "I love you," I whispered. "You *are* my mother. Full stop."

She kissed my cheek. "I told you. No matter what."

I glanced at Dad and caught him wiping his eyes. He tossed his tissue in the trash. "Now, we can go home." He hugged me. "Love you, son."

"Love you, too, Dad."

Ma grinned. "Since we have the church, did you and Sasha want to walk down that aisle?"

"Nah, Ma."I shook my head. "We're not there yet."

"What happened?" Dad asked.

I didn't want to get into it again, so I told him, "I am who I am."

He barked out a laugh. "Well, you're also my son. And I don't run away from shit."

Ma gasped. "Stew! We're in the church."

Dad dropped his head and grumbled. "Sorry, Lord." He cleared his throat. "Anyway, if she'll hear you, talk to her."

"I don't even know if Sasha's coming."

"She got here about ten minutes ago," Ma said.

My eyes flashed to hers. "You saw her?"

"Yeah. She came in looking stunning in yellow, with the beautiful Ms. Ashlyn. She should be in the sanctuary. I told her—"

I'd walked to the door before I realized what I'd done. I stopped, rushed back over to Ma, kissed her cheek, and gave Dad dap. "I have to go. We'll talk later."

When I entered the church foyer, people were exiting the church in a single file. Bliss must've already made the announcement. I waited, hoping to catch Sasha before she left. Several of the church ladies stopped me on their way out to ask where my mother was, but I'd shrugged them off. I figured Ma would appreciate my evasiveness today.

Duke walked over to me. "You missed it. Blake felt bad leaving Bliss to make the announcement."

I shot him a sidelong glance. "What did she do?"

"She went on the wedding website and emailed all the guests. It was like a domino effect. By the time Bliss made it up to the front of the church, most of the people already knew."

Laughing, I shook my head at my sister's antics. "That's creative."

"Anyway, we're headed over to the reception. You coming? Blake and Lennox may show up after all, already married."

"This is Blake we're talking about, right?"

"Right. At least we'll eat good." He left me standing there.

"Dad!" Raven waved at me as she exited the church. She pointed behind her. "I have Ashlyn. See you at the reception."

My gaze followed Raven's finger and Ashlyn grinned at me.

"You got this." Ashlyn gave me a thumbs-up, then pointed behind her before walking outside.

Then Sasha emerged from the sanctuary. Ma was right. She was stunning. The short dress and strappy sandals she wore accentuated her long legs. Her long hair was straight, flowing down her back. She was laughing at something Bishop said, but when she saw me, her smile fell.

I approached her tentatively. "Hey."

She sucked in a deep breath. "Hi."

"Thanks for coming."

"Honestly, I probably shouldn't have. We still have a lot to discuss," she said. "I don't want to pretend to be okay, but I'm—"

I captured her lips with mine, pulling her to me and kissing her fully. Talking wasn't my strong suit, but we had always communicated with more than words, so I poured all the love, the adoration, the respect, and even the desperation I felt for her into the kiss. It didn't matter that people were watching. It didn't matter that we were in the church. The only thing that mattered was us. "Please," I murmured against her mouth. "I'll talk to you every minute of every day. Just don't leave."

"Tristan." She pulled back, tears standing in her eyes. Dropping her head onto my chest, she nodded. "Okay. Let's go."

Chapter Sixteen

SUDDENLY

Sasha

*W*hen I was a kid, I wanted to be a successful career woman. Two kids. A loving husband who worked all day. A dog. A big house with a swing on the porch. As I grew up, my goals changed. I still wanted a career. But my focus was on being self-sufficient. I wanted to be able to support myself. No kids. No husband. Just a luxury car, a fabulous crib, and companionship when *I* wanted it. Basically, I wanted to be Hilary Banks from *The Fresh Prince of Bel-Air*.

But life … Nothing ever really turned out how I expected. It also didn't turn out as bad as it could've. While I wasn't raised in a mansion, surrounded by sitcom parents who doled out important lessons every thirty minutes, I did have support. My support came through my siblings, a school nurse who risked her job to save us, a madam who broke the law but was loyal to a fault, a friend whose family had odd similarities to the ones in my favorite TV shows ... And Tristan.

I wasn't super spiritual, but I believed in God. And I absolutely believed that He sent Tristan to me. And I didn't realize that until now. Until he kissed me so long and so hard in the middle of the church foyer and then begged me not to leave him.

The truth was I couldn't leave him even if I wanted to. Because he owned my heart. I had no idea I could love someone so deeply, so completely. I didn't think that I would meet someone who loved my daughter like his own. I wasn't prepared to let that go. *Ever.*

"I'm sorry," he whispered.

We were sitting in someone's car outside of the hotel where the reception was supposed to take place. It wasn't the rental, but I trusted that he didn't steal a vehicle. The sweltering heat of yesterday had passed and we were blessed with a nice August day. The soft breeze floated through the car, tickling my skin.

I shifted in my seat. "Tristan, I want you to know that I do understand why you didn't tell me the truth then." Of course I did. He didn't know me, and he was protective of his family. "If I were in your shoes, I probably wouldn't have said anything either."

"I didn't expect to like you," he admitted.

Unable to help myself, I giggled. "I'm sorry, but that's so funny. Did you expect to hate me?"

He smiled. "Not really. I didn't expect to feel anything. I never had before. But you challenged me, you made me look in the mirror at myself. Then, I knew I needed more of you. I thought I'd been in love before, but there is nothing and no one that comes close to what I feel for you."

"I want to be with you, Tristan. But I'd be lying if I

told you that I wasn't worried that another secret, another Britt, was going to come out of the shadows and destroy everything." My voice cracked and I counted to ten, blowing out a deep breath. "I need to be able to trust that we're in this together. Meaning, no matter what, we're honest with each other. Because it's not just me that I have to consider. Ashlyn loves you like a father."

On the way to the church, Ashlyn told me about her talk with Tristan earlier. I was dumbfounded at the revelation that she'd secretly called him Dad when nobody could hear her. When she talked to her friends, she referred to him as Papa.

"She told me," he confessed.

"So you know this is not a game. I'm her mother. My job is to protect her, and I will burn everything to the ground to do it."

"I feel the same. Ashlyn *is* my daughter, and that wouldn't change even if you decide that you can't be with me."

"I'm not making that choice." Feeling a need to close the distance between us, literally and figuratively, I climbed over the middle console and sat in his lap. Brushing my lips over his, I whispered, "I choose you. Every day."

He gripped my chin in his palm and kissed me. "I love you, Sasha. Not just for now. Forever."

His words washed over me, and I embraced him, clinging to him as if he controlled my next breath. "Love you, too."

The sound of someone knocking on the window startled me, and I jerked up, hitting my head on the roof of the car. "Shit."

Tristan rubbed the top of my head as he glared at Asa. "Bruh, what's up?"

"How are you gon' kick me out of my truck? I had to

catch a ride with Sister Holbrook. She kept trying to show me pictures of her granddaughter."

"You know I gave Blake and Lennox my shit," Tristan said.

Asa pinched the bridge of his nose. "You're going to have to take Blake's car home, man. I have somewhere to be."

"Yeah, I'll just go steal the party bus they rented to transport them for the day," Tristan said, sarcasm dripping from his tone.

"I don't know what to tell you." Asa tried the door, but it was locked. "Bruh? Really?"

"Shouldn't you be inside?" Tristan asked.

"I have to make a run," Asa insisted.

I covered Tristan's mouth and addressed Asa. "We'll be done in a minute."

"Walk away," Tristan added.

Asa stepped back, grumbling a slew of curses. "I'll be back."

Once we were alone again, Tristan sighed. "I don't know what's going on with him."

I tilted my head, assessing him. "Are you worried about him?"

"He mentioned something about situation he was in a couple of months ago. When I called him, he acted like everything was good."

"Maybe you should talk to him. It worked with Duke."

He chuckled. "I'll hang out with him soon."

I rested my head on his shoulder. "I guess we better go in."

"I'll see if I can find someone's car. How did you get to the church?"

Leah had dropped us off on her way to the airport. "She told me I should tell you to watch your back."

Tristan laughed then. "I don't doubt it."

"Actually, she was the voice of reason last night."

"Then I need to thank her."

I ran my fingers over the back of his head. "I don't want us to go through this again, Tristan. If there's anything you haven't told me, please just say it."

"Truthfully, there's a lot I haven't told you—about my past, about my life. But if you're referring things that impact you directly ... Nothing."

"I can accept that." Despite our history, there were things I still hadn't shared with him. I'd only scratched the surface on Marlon. But I hoped that when we both felt comfortable enough to reveal the missing pieces, that we'd continue to offer each other understanding and unwavering support.

My phone buzzed. I checked the screen and giggled, holding it up for Tristan to read.

Ashlyn: **I hope you're making up. If not, don't come in.**

I typed out a response, letting Tristan read it before I hit SEND.

You better stop talking to me like I'm one of yo' lil friends.

We got out of the truck and walked up to the door, hand-in-hand. Stopping at the door, he peered down at me, his love for me evident in his dark eyes. "I love you," he whispered.

I winked. "Good to know. Ready to do this?"

"Forever."

———

Tristan

199

. . .

Two Months Later

"I love it." Sasha beamed up at me as she traced the edge of the painting. "I can't believe you did this for me."

For the last few weeks, Sasha had been working long hours, as her main business kicked up before the holidays. In addition, her first several tenants had moved into Ash Falls Community, so she'd wanted to be on site to welcome them there. She'd complained about not having enough time for herself. So I'd done my best to give her what she needed.

We started the day with breakfast at her favorite restaurant, followed by a trip to the spa. While she got the works —a full-body massage, a deluxe pedicure, and a manicure —I was busy getting everything ready for her.

Once she emerged from the spa rejuvenated, I surprised her with tickets to the new exhibit at the Museum of Contemporary Art. One of her favorite artists was showing there, and I'd arranged to purchase one of the pieces she'd been looking at. We ended the night with dinner and music at Rock Steady Atlanta.

She finally set the painting down, turning to me with a wicked gleam in her eyes. She removed her belt and her dress fell to the floor. I let my gaze rake over her body, lingering on her breasts in the black lace bra and traveling down to her matching thong.

After sauntering over to me, she climbed on my lap. "You really do spoil me."

I slid my hand up her spine, wrapping my hand around her neck and tugging her to me. "You deserve it," I murmured against her mouth, before dipping my tongue inside and kissing her.

Sasha unbuttoned my shirt, struggling with the last button before she yanked it off, ripping out two of the buttons. The sound of them hitting the hard wood echoed in the room. "Shit," She bit down on my bottom lip. "Sorry," she breathed.

I ran my finger over her slit. "I didn't like that shirt anyway."

She laughed, tugging at my earlobe with her teeth. "Hey. I picked it out."

"I know." I pinched her clit, before inching one finger inside of her. "You're so wet, baby."

"Only for you." She rocked into me, her breath hitching in her throat as she climbed higher. Then higher. When she came, she threw her head back as she trembled above me.

"I can't get enough of you," I whispered against her skin, licking the sheen of sweat between her breasts. "I want to stay here forever."

She moaned. "Yes. More."

"Whatever you need." Lifting up, I took my pants and boxers off. "I'm always here to give you what you need."

She lowered herself onto my dick and smirked. "Good to know."

We made love, lips pressed together, bodies moving in sync. Harder. Deeper. Faster. Healing each other. Fusing the missing pieces of ourselves back together. Being with her like this, loving on her was one of my favorite things to do. Better than rock climbing. Better than gaming. Better than work. Better than anything. Better than everything.

Sasha came first, holding me to her as she shuddered over me, wringing me dry. I was right behind her, growling her name as I followed her over.

She sagged into me. "Tristan," she whispered, trailing kisses over my jaw to my ear. "Again."

I lifted her in my arms and dropped her onto the mattress. "As you wish."

After we made love again, I fell back onto the bed, pulling her into me. "I love this," I said, pressing my lips to her temple.

"I'll be glad when you love it enough to get some furniture." She cracked up. "It's way past time."

I chuckled, tickling her. "You're silly for that." I'd never laughed as much as I did with Sasha. Experiencing life with her and Ashlyn had changed everything for me—for the better.

She perched herself on an elbow. "Seriously, Tristan. Can you stay a while? You're living like you still plan to move soon."

I stared into her brown eyes. "I am."

Frowning, she said, "Where are you moving?"

Initially, we'd decided to table the discussion about moving in until Ashlyn graduated. But I was ready to take that step with her. I wanted to spend every day with my family, every night with her. "Wherever you are."

Her expression softened. "What happened to waiting? Do you think it's too soon?"

"I'm just *waiting* on you to give me the word."

She brushed her thumb over my bottom lip, placing a sweet kiss to my mouth. "After you left last night, I talked to Ashlyn. We both agreed that this arrangement—with you moving back here and us going back and forth between houses—wouldn't work long term. I called Ola and asked if she would take a job as the property manager of Ash Falls. Because I couldn't stay there anymore. Not without you."

"That's all I needed to hear. Now, let's go buy some furniture."

She hugged me. "I love you so much."

"Good to know. I love you, too."

As we made plans to step into the next phase of our relationship, I didn't regret anything about our history, not even my past because it brought me to her. And after running from myself and from others for so long, I was ready to stop. Because I'd found my safe place in her.

Where It Ends ... Maybe?

Epilogue

WITH YOU I'M BORN AGAIN

Tristan

Thanksgiving Day, This Year

For the first time ever, I celebrated Thanksgiving twice—first with my family and now with Sasha's family. Thankfully, Daphne had taken pity on us and made Surf n' Turf, instead of the traditional turkey and dressing.

Vincent and Josslyn couldn't make it this year, but they all agreed to try again next year. Since the summer, Ashlyn had grown extremely close to her cousins. She was even considering attending Wayne State University, where Nero was an associate professor at the medical school.

Daphne emerged from the kitchen, two beers in hand. She handed one to Nero first, then me. "Who's winning?"

"How's the new house?" Nero asked, ignoring her. He'd been cursing at the TV the entire first half because the Lions hadn't scored a touchdown yet.

"We move in next month," I announced.

After we'd made the decision to move in together, we didn't waste any time. I sold my place and we purchased a four-bedroom house. The goal was to have plenty of room for Ashlyn and even Raven when she wanted to stay the night. And Sasha wanted an extra bedroom for family. Because she always wanted to be able to offer someone a place to stay if they needed it.

Sasha squeezed my leg under the table. "We love it. After we close, I want you to visit."

Daphne and Sasha started making plans for a visit next month around the holidays, while Nero and I forced our attention back on the game.

"Damn," Nero shouted, when our quarterback got sacked. "This is some bullshit."

"See!" Daphne shook her head with disgust. "This is what I'm talking about."

Sasha and I glanced at each other. She mouthed, 'I'm hungry.'

But I knew that dinner would not be served until after the game. That's just how it went for diehard fans. And I totally understood the sentiment because I was one of those fans myself. Blue and white, through and through.

"Anyway," Daphne turned to us, "did your brother tell you he proposed to me?"

Sasha's mouth fell open. "What? No."

"That's because she turned me down," Nero explained.

Daphne rolled her eyes. "Because we said we didn't need to get married."

Sasha and I hadn't talked about marriage either, but I'd thought about it. Ashlyn had been hinting around, along with Ola, my parents, and Bliss. Yet, Sasha had stayed quiet on the matter.

Curious, I asked, "Why don't you want to get married?"

Shrugging, Daphne sipped her wine. "I just don't think it's necessary."

"Right," Sasha agreed.

I shot her a sidelong glance. "Is that what you believe?"

Sasha blinked. "Huh?"

I looked at Nero and Daphne, who were watching us intently, before turning my attention back to Sasha. "You don't believe in marriage?"

"Baby, of course I do," she assured me. "I just don't think it's a necessary, or even obvious, step in a relationship. As long as two people know who they are to each other, they should be good."

Daphne nodded. "Exactly."

"Whatever," Nero grumbled.

"So you'd never get married?" I asked Sasha.

Sasha frowned. "I didn't say that. You asked if I believed in marriage. And I do."

"Would you marry me?"

Daphne gasped, but I didn't take my eyes off Sasha.

With wide eyes, Sasha asked, "Is that a question? Or *the* question?"

I shifted in my seat. "Just curious. We've never had the discussion before."

"Oh." She bit into a chip, eyeing me suspiciously.

The doorbell rang and Daphne rushed to the front of the house. Nero followed her.

Sasha turned to me. "What the hell was that?"

"What?" I asked, playing dumb. I didn't even know why I'd asked the question. It wasn't like I was ready to propose.

Or am I?

"You've never brought up marriage before?" she whisper-yelled. "Why do it now?"

"I just wondered what you thought about it."

"Do you want to propose?"

"Not like this," I argued. "Shit. It was question." And I was a punk.

"Fine." She huffed, folding her arms over her chest. "For future reference, though, if you were to propose, I don't need a spectacle and I do not want you to do it in front of other people." She kissed me, then ate another chip. "That's all you need to know."

I smiled, chuckling at her roundabout way of telling me that she'd be open to marriage. "I love you," I said.

"Good to know."

"Wait." Daphne's voiced carried through the front of the office. "Don't—"

Seconds later, Britt walked into the living room. "I need to talk to you."

I jumped up. "Not here. Not today."

Britt nodded toward Sasha. "Not you, Tristan. Her."

Sasha stood slowly. "What could you have to talk to me about?"

"I saw him," she breathed, as fresh tears spilled from her eyes. "Marlon is alive. And I figured you should know because you're the only other person that probably wants him dead more than me."

———

ASA got next! Subscribe to my Newsletter to be the first to know about Young Family news!

Young in Love Series

Her Little Secret (Prelude)
It's Not Me, It's You
It's Not Love, It's Business
It's Not the Hookup, It's the Chase
It's Not Them, It's Only Her
It's Not Forever, It's For Now

In the meantime... Keep reading for an excerpt from
Smoke in Love. Alaiya Young is a relative.

Excerpt: Smoke in Love

FOUR20 BAE

Spencer

Twenty-Five Years Ago

The eerie silence should've been my first clue that something was up, but I entered the crowded house anyway. Scanning the room, I made eye contact with every muthafucka there. The threat was unspoken, they knew what was up. I never had to say a word.

"Where is she?" I grumbled.

My homeboy, O, pointed to the hallway leading to the bedrooms. "Man, I didn't give it to her."

My jaw clenched, and I fought the urge to fuck that nigga up. Slowly, I blew out a breath. "Who did?"

Oscar didn't say anything, but I followed his gaze to the culprit. Without another word, I stomped over to that punk-ass fool, Fred, and hemmed him up against the wall.

"Tell me why I shouldn't break every damn bone in your body right now."

"I'm not— Man, stop. I didn't d-do anything," Fred stammered, "she's a grown-ass woman. How was I supposed to know?"

Gripping his shirt harder, I pulled back, then slammed him against the wall. "I made it clear a long time ago that if you fuck with Laiya, I will fuck you up."

"She's not hurt." Fred's sister, Shaunie, stood at the door of the kitchen, a bottle of water in hand. "I made her lay down. But he's right. What we look like tellin' a groan-ass woman she can't do what the hell she wants to do?"

Even with her assurances, even though she made a valid point, the rage building inside of me hadn't waned. "Shaunie, I don't want to hear that shit. Someone called me and told me she was in trouble. When I got here, muthafuckas lookin' at me like somebody did something to her. How you think I'm supposed to react?"

"Calm yo' ass down, then," she said, walking over to me. "I told you ... she's fine." She motioned to my fists. "You gon' let him go now?"

Reluctantly, I released him. Turning to the fellas in the room, I gestured to the door. "All y'all can get the fuck out."

Shaunie planted a hand on her hips. "Nigga, this is *my* house."

"You must've misunderstood me," I told her. "You might pay the rent here, but I own this shit."

"What the fuck?" she exclaimed, flailing her hands in the air.

But I was already on my way to the bedroom. "Now," I clarified.

"For *her*?" Shaunie shouted.

I stilled, that question giving me pause. Slowly, I turned

to face her. The past between me and Shaunie was volatile, rocky. Toxic relationship? That was us. Until I ended it. It wasn't the fact that she was questioning me, it was the way she said "*her*" that tripped me out. Almost like she was jealous. And since I knew her to be a vindictive woman, I wanted to make it clear that Alaiya was off limits to her, too. "What did you say?" I challenged, my voice low. "You want to repeat that?"

Shaunie swallowed visibly. "I'm just sayin'," she murmured. "Please don't do this."

Technically, I *could* terminate her lease. Shaunie wasn't the biggest weed dealer in the community, but at first glance, I definitely had "just cause" to evict with all the visible drug paraphernalia at the crib.

"Are you really doing this?" she asked, worry lining her features. "You know I would've never let anything happen to her."

She looked sincere enough, but I could never tell with Shaunie. One minute, she was the nicest person in the room. The next she was a damn demon in disguise. At the same time, I knew she needed the spot. She had two little kids, who I hoped were with her mother right now. "Where are the boys?"

Shaunie blinked, obviously thrown off by the change of subject. "With my mom."

"Good." I let out a heavy sigh. "The noise complaints, the parties, the strange cars parked on the street … I could make you leave, but I won't. Today. But consider this a warning."

"Oh," she crossed her arms over her chest, "so you're too good for us now? Your brother is running for office, and you want to distance yourself from the hood politics?"

"I'll never forget where I came from. But I *will* protect

my investment." I picked up the roach clip from the table and held it up. "I don't care who you are."

"You're acting like you don't smoke."

Shrugging, I tossed the metal into a small trashcan. "Maybe I'm just tired of your bullshit? The only reason you're still here is because of those boys. I want them to have a home. But don't try me."

Without another word, I stomped down the hallway to the main bedroom. I didn't need directions because I knew where it was. After all, I'd lived in the house when I was with Shaunie. Painted the walls, laid the floors, remodeled the bathrooms …

When I stopped in front of the door, I turned to find Shaunie watching me intently. She didn't speak, but the question was in her eyes. Eventually, though, she walked away shaking her head. Then, I let myself into the room.

I spotted her right away, splayed out on the mattress, face down. "Laiya," I called.

"Huh?" she grunted, then let out a whimper.

I stared down at her. I brushed a strand of hair from her face, then smoothed my thumb over her furrowed brow. It was the closest I'd ever gotten to her bare skin. Because it was rare that we touched each other at all. A brief hug every so often, but that was the extent of our physical contact. Her eyes were closed, and she looked like an angel. Like I'd just got a glimpse of Heaven.

"Hey." I nudged her. "I need you to wake up."

One eye popped open. "Spencer? It's you?"

I smiled. "Yeah, I'm here."

"You're here to save me?" she whispered.

"I should let your butt stay here," I teased. "I told you not to come."

She giggled. "And I told you not to tell me what to do."

Earlier that morning, I'd run into her at Luca's Coney

Island. She'd mentioned going to the party, but I warned her against it. It had been a long time since I'd attended one of Shaunie's sets, but nothing ever changed. Loud music. Drinks. Drugs. Dancing. Fights. Good thing I got there before all hell broke loose.

With a heavy sigh, I picked her up, cradling her in my arms. She smelled like snow, so crisp, but slightly sweet. I wanted to bury my nose in her hair, in her neck. "Where's your purse?"

Curling into me, she mumbled, "I don't know. Probably out there." She frowned. "I think I gave it to Shaunie."

"How did you get here?"

"I drove."

Shit.

"Spence?" She lifted her head up, meeting my gaze. "Is it normal to not feel my face?"

"They don't call that bong *Lucifer* for no reason."

"Don't remind me. I couldn't stop coughing. I ate a whole box of Frosted Flakes."

Chuckling, I said, "That's a lot."

"I'm never doing this again," she promised.

"Good. Now, let's get you out of here."

As I carried her toward the front of the house, I asked Shaunie to bring me her purse and told O to make sure her car stayed where it was. When Fred opened the front door for me, Rodger Mills was standing there.

Figures.

He frowned. "What are you doing?"

"Taking her home."

Laiya lifted her head again. "Rod? What are you doing here?"

"I came to get you," he said. "Shaunie called me."

I whirled around to face Shaunie, but she wasn't quick

enough to wipe that smirk off her face. She shrugged. "I figured her *man* should know what happened."

Rod held his arms out. "I'll take her."

"You should've been here with her," I snapped.

"I had to work," he explained unnecessarily. I didn't give a fuck about his excuses. "She's my girlfriend. *I* got her."

I glanced down at Laiya. For the first time tonight, her eyes were clear and locked on mine. "You want to go with him?" I asked.

Her eyes fluttered closed and her head fell against my shoulder. To any observer, they might've thought she was just high. But I knew her … If she wanted to go with him, she would've made it more than clear.

"Laiya?" Rod called. "Come on."

Decision made, I looked at him. "Nah, man. I'll take her home. You can meet us there."

Recommended Reading

MEET THE YOUNG FAMILY

It's Not Forever, It's For Now is the fifth book in my Young in Love Series, but the Young family has been cutting up for a long time! If you'd like to get acquainted with this family before you read, I recommend starting with the following books:

Paityn Young found everlasting love in my prelude novella, HER LITTLE SECRET.

IT'S NOT ME, IT'S YOU is book one in the Young In Love Series, followed by IT'S NOT LOVE, IT'S BUSINESS, then IT'S NOT THE HOOKUP, IT'S THE CHASE, and IT'S NOT THEM, IT'S ONLY HER.

———

Want more of the Youngs?

Blake Young appeared as Ryleigh's friend in my Once Upon a Baby novella, BEYOND EVER AFTER.

Duke Young burst onto the scene in my Pure Talent novels, THE WAY YOU TEMPT ME and THE WAY YOU HOLD ME. And he stole the show.

Dallas Young made her presence known in my Once Upon a Funeral novella, FINDING COOPER.

Duke and Bliss also made an appearance in my novella, SOME KIND OF LOVE.

———

Meet their extended family in TEN CHRISTMAS SHOTS, which is a follow-up of my first historical romance set in the 1980s, MADE TO HOLD YOU.

Also, did you know that there was another set of Youngs? Yes, you heard that right. Aunt Vicki married someone with her same last name.

I introduced that side of the family in SMOKE IN LOVE, THE SECRETS WE HATE, and THE SECRETS WE CREATE - KNOX.

Please Note: Several of these stories take place around the same time. Some events may happen in multiple books from a different POV.

www.ellewright.com

Wait a Minute. Is that...?

After all this time … YES! That is THE Den from my Edge of
Scandal Series!!!

If you want to know how Caden Smith lost everything, dive into
this series: THE FORBIDDEN MAN, HIS ALL NIGHT, HER
KIND OF MAN, and ALL HE WANTS FOR CHRISTMAS.

Is it finally time for him to get his story? We shall see.

Also … are you wondering who Britt is? She's not new to the
canvas.

Nero and Daphne were featured in my *Mr. Down for
Whatever,* which was part of the Baes of Juneteenth Series. I
introduced Britt in this book.

If you haven't already read it, now is a good time to start. If you
can't already tell … she will be back!

———

Acknowledgments

I'm so grateful! God has been good to me!

To my family and my "Framily", I love you all. Thanks for supporting me through everything.

A special shout-out to the awesome readers , bloggers, and writers that I've met on this journey. Thanks for your support. I appreciate you!

Connect with Elle!

Thank you for reading Tristan and Sasha's story! I love to hear from my readers. If you enjoyed *It's Not Forever, It's For Now*, please consider posting a review or sending an email. They really do help. Don't forget to tell your friends!

Subscribe to my Newsletter
New Releases, Upcoming projects, and Freebies!

On Facebook,
Join my cocktail lounge for exclusive updates, drink recipes, and lots of fun!
bit.ly/EllesCocktailLounge

Visit my website: www.ellewright.com

Email me at info@ellewright.com

facebook.com/ellewrightauthor
instagram.com/lwrightauthor
amazon.com/Elle-Wright/e/B00VMEWB78
bookbub.com/profile/elle-wright

Also by Elle Wright

Contemporary Romance

Young In Love Series

(Very large family + Layered characters + Lots of heat + Laugh
out loud moments)

Her Little Secret (Prelude)

It's Not Me, It's You

It's Not Love, It's Business

It's Not the Hookup, It's the Chase

It's Not Them, It's Only Her

It's Not Forever, It's For Now

Smoke and Burn Series

(Smoking' Hot Heroes + steamy scenes + Lots of humor)

Some Kind of Love

Edge of Scandal Series

(Edgy contemporary romance + Heat + Humor + Scandal)

The Forbidden Man

His All Night

Her Kind of Man

All He Wants for Christmas

Wellspring Series

(Small Town Romance + Angst + Twists and Turns + Humor)

Touched By You

Enticed By You

Pleasured By You

Pure Talent Series

(Sexy + Steamy moments + High-powered executives + Drama)

The Way You Tempt Me

The Way You Hold Me

The Way You Love Me

Once Upon a Series

Beyond Forever (Once Upon a Bridesmaid)

Beyond Ever After (Once Upon a Baby)

Finding Cooper (Once Upon a Funeral)

The Secrets We Hate (Once Upon a Murder)

The Secrets We Create - Knox (Once Upon a Murder)

Standalones

The Closing Bid

Irresistible Temptation

The Baes

One More Drink

Ten Christmas Shots

Mr. Down for Whatever

Smoke in Love

Historical Romance

Made To Hold You (The 80s)

Suspense/Thriller

Basement Level 5: Never Scared

About the Author

There was never a time when Elle Wright wasn't about to start a book, wasn't already deep in a book—or had just finished one. She grew up believing in the importance of reading, and became a lover of all things romance when her mother gave her her first romance novel. She lives in Michigan.

Connect with Elle!
www.ellewright.com
info@ellewright.com